Shadow Boxing

A Tom Donavan Mystery

David Coleman

NFB
<<<>>>
Buffalo, NY

For Paul, Joe and Jim and three lifetimes

worth of stories.

And the real life "Big Tom."

You left quite an impression

Shadow Boxing

*To Mark,
Thank you
I hope you enjoy
this.*

David Coleman

<<<>>>

Chapter 1

Tom put the case on the shelf in front of him and popped the clasp. He opened the lid and looked at the brand new Glock 17 G4.

"Nice," Sherry Palkowski said.

Sherry worked with Tom at Frederickson and Associates, a private investigation firm in Buffalo, NY. She had also helped him out of a jam nine months before when he was trying to locate the missing wife of a local real estate magnate and landed on the wrong side of the husband's more questionable business dealings. Sherry had disabled a man who had been pointing a shotgun at them and then shot and killed one of the man's watchdogs. Since then they had become good friends, with Tom spending time with Sherry and her partner, Amber, outside of work.

They were at an indoor shooting range in Tonawanda. Tom had recently received his carry permit from the State of New York and purchased the pistol and a box of shells. He picked up the ammunition jacket and started to load it.

"How about a little friendly wager?" Sherry asked.

"Not to be a little bitch, but it's been a while since I've fired a weapon."

Sherry smiled. "Alright. I'll spot you a few points if you're going to try to sandbag me."

Tom popped the magazine into the butt of the Glock and set it down on the shelf in front of him. He picked up his ear and eye protection and said, "Okay big shot. Loser buys the first round." He noticed he suddenly had a knot in his stomach.

Sherry disappeared, heading back towards her spot on the range and Tom picked up the pistol. He thumbed off the safety and chambered a round. Suddenly he noticed that his hand was shaking involuntarily. He tried to steady it with some success but when he looked down the range at the paper target hanging ten yards away he noticed his vision had blurred slightly. He heard Sherry's pistol go off from somewhere to his right, seven evenly spaced shots. He blinked his eyes and tried to focus. Using all his concentration he aimed, took a deep breath and as he exhaled he squeezed the trigger. He squinted and confirmed to himself that he had missed the target completely.

The indoor range was cool and yet he could feel himself perspiring through his undershirt. He raised the pistol again and his hands resumed shaking. As hard as he tried to relax he couldn't seem to steady himself and the knot in his stomach became more acute. He fired three more times, only two of his shots hitting the paper target and neither one close to the marked area. He put the safety back on and set the pistol down in front of him. He took of his eye protection and wiped his brow.

"You okay?" Tom turned around and saw Sherry standing behind him with a concerned look on her face.

Tom respected Sherry too much to lie to her. "I dunno, I'm a little shaky," he said.

"I heard you stop and I thought maybe you were having a problem with your gun. But Jesus Tom, you're as white as a sheet."

The last time Tom had fired a weapon was almost three years previously. That night, he had killed two men, one of them a DEA agent and the other one an unarmed drug dealer. The shooting had ended Tom's ten-year career with the Buffalo Police Department. He had carried an unlicensed gun during the Shield's case last year, but hadn't come close to considering firing it.

He was embarrassed and angry that he couldn't control his own body. He had waited two years to get his carry permit; in his current line of work it wasn't a bad idea to carry protection. He often thought about that fateful night at the housing project that ended his career as a policeman but had never considered that there could be this kind of residual effect.

Sherry seemed to understand what was happening. "Did you ever talk to anybody about it?"

"You mean like a shrink?"

"Doesn't the department provide counseling after an officer- involved shooting?"

Tom had started to break down the Glock. He shrugged and said, "I had one session with the department psychiatrist and then I was off the force."

They stood quiet for a moment and then Sherry asked, "Do you think it could be Post Traumatic Stress Disorder?"

"Could be a bad hot dog."

"Seriously Tom, my cousin came back from two tours in Afghanistan and I could tell he was different. On the surface he was still all tough-guy Marine, but underneath he was dealing with some issues."

"What did he do?"

"He got counseling through the VA and he goes to a support group with other veterans."

Tom had finished packing up. His heart rate had returned to normal. He looked at Sherry and said, "I'll be okay Sher'. This is my first time out and maybe I wasn't ready."

She frowned and said, "Don't get me wrong, but you shouldn't-"

"Sherry I'm fine," he interrupted.

Without a word they walked out of the range and Tom went to the locker room and splashed cold water on his face. He gave himself a moment and then went out to the lobby where Sherry stood looking slightly cross.

Tom exhaled and said, "I'm sorry I snapped in there. I've always had a hard time accepting my shortcomings."

Sherry's face lost some of its tension and she said, "I wasn't trying to imply that you're crazy. I was just implying that you're too much of a stubborn asshole to reach out when you need help. You're not the first person who's gone through this."

Tom thought about that for a second and said, "Fair enough. And thanks."

As they left the building into the early April chill Sherry seemed to be thinking about something. Tom picked up on it and said, "What?"

She hesitated and started, "This probably isn't the best time..."

"What is it?"

She smiled and blushed slightly. "I got into the Academy," she said.

Tom turned and looked at her and said, "Sherry, that's fantastic."

She had taken the police exam several months before and had done very well on it. At first, before they had gotten to know each other, the topic of her becoming a police officer had been one they chose not to discuss. Tom assumed Sherry kept her distance from him because of the way his career had ended while Sherry assumed he was bitter and would resent her for it. Neither scenario had proven to be true.

Now her face lit up in a broad smile. "Thanks, Tom."

"Did you tell Cal yet?" He asked. Cal Frederickson was their boss, the head of Frederickson and Associates.

She shook her head. "First thing tomorrow. I just found out this morning and I've been just about ready to bust open."

Tom took a step forward and gave her a hug. "That is fantastic," he said. "You are going to make a great cop."

"Thank you so much Tom. The next class starts in five weeks so we still have some time to get into trouble."

They broke off their embrace and looked at each other. Tom finally said, "And I just got you broken in. Now I'm going to have to share an office with some stranger. Probably another overweight ex-cop like Adams or Willis."

"You don't know that. It could be another fascinating young lady like me. Maybe even a straight one this time."

Tom felt himself blush slightly. He offered to buy Sherry the beer he said he owed her but she let him off the hook and said she had to go tell her father the news. They said goodbye and Tom headed off to his car.

As the engine was warming up he took his cell phone out of his coat pocket and noticed he had received a voicemail while they were on the range. He checked the caller ID and saw that it came from a number he didn't recognize. He called voicemail and punched in his access code.

The playback started, "Um... yes... this is a message for Tom Donovan. Ah... Mr. Donovan this is Father William Stepniak from Roswell Park. If you could give me a call at..." the priest went on and gave his number, with the extension and then rang off.

The call had come from the Roswell Park Cancer Institute. Tom had never heard of a Father Stepniak before or had any idea why he would be calling. His curiosity got the better of him so he dialed the number immediately. After the second ring a female voice answered, "Thank you for calling the Roswell Park Pastoral Care Office. How may I direct your call?"

"This is Tom Donovan, I am returning Father Stepniak's call."

"One moment please, I'll see if he's in."

Tom was on hold for a few minutes and then Father Stepniak came on. "Mr. Donovan?" he said.

"Yes, Father. I'm returning your call."

"Oh, sorry about the message I left," the priest said. "I'm afraid I still get tongue-tied when I have to leave a message."

"That's alright Father," Tom was hoping this wasn't just some kind of fund raising call but didn't want to be rude and tell the priest to cut the small talk.

"Mr. Donovan, I have been asked to reach out to you by a friend of yours, Henry Loughran."

"Hank?"

"Pardon me?"

"Sorry Father," Tom said, "I have always known him as Hank."

"Ah yes, of course.   Mr. Loughran is a patient here and asked me to try to get a message to you. I'm afraid he's pretty far along in his battle with lung cancer and he expressed a desire to talk to you."

Tom tried to let it sink in. Hank "Lights Out" Loughran had been his trainer when Tom was a teenager preparing for the Gold Gloves. Hank had always seemed to have a cigarette in his mouth or behind his ear. He would have to be in his seventies now and Tom wondered how he had survived this long.

"Of course, Father.   I'll head right over there," Tom said pulling out a notebook. "Could you give me Mr. Loughran's room number?"

Chapter 2

Donovan, freshly showered and changed, arrived at Roswell Park just before 7:00 PM. He got a visitor's pass in the lobby and made his way up to the fifth floor and found his way to Hank Loughran's room.

A wave of guilt washed over him as he looked at his old mentor. He hadn't spoken to Hank in over a year and he had no idea Hank had been sick. Hank's once athletic body had been wasted by cancer. Father Stepniak had warned Tom over the phone that Hank was in a bad way, including the fact that Hank's face and neck were swollen from the steroids he had been given as part of his treatment. Other than that Tom couldn't help but notice that underneath the hospital linens there wasn't much left to Hank.

Hank "Lights Out" Loughran had been a professional boxer from the late fifties to the mid-sixties. He retired with a record of 32 wins and 12 losses. During his last professional fight, against a middleweight named Ozzie Jefferson, Hank suffered an eye injury that would later be diagnosed as a detached retina and lost on a TKO. Ironically Jefferson's career would come to an abrupt end a few months later when his body was found in the Charles River. The rumor was that he had crossed somebody in the Boston mob. Hank came home to Buffalo and got a job at Bethlehem Steel, but, never really able to get boxing out of his system, he founded the Southside Athletic Club, where he trained fighters for the next thirty years. One of his most promising charges had been Tom's father, who won the Buffalo Gold Gloves heavyweight title in 1979.

Hank stirred suddenly while Tom was standing over the bed and slowly opened his watery eyes. It took a moment but then he seemed to focus and recognize his former pupil.

"Tommy," he rasped.

"Hiya Hank, good to see you."

Hank coughed and his body shook. He had oxygen going in to his nose but it sounded as if he were struggling to breathe. "I know I've never looked better," he said.

"Hank, I am so sorry, I had no idea..."

Hank raised the arm that didn't have an intravenous needle in it as if to wave Tom off. "Don't worry about it kid. Whitey Brennan tells me you have had a full plate lately."

"Still, I wish I would have known."

"Hey you're here now." Another cough.

"What are your doctors saying?"

"Ha, they say I'll be running marathons next month," Hank said with a smile. Tom wasn't sure how to react so he smiled back. Hank weakly adjusted himself in his bed so he could look at Tom directly and then said, "A month or two. They want the bed so they're shipping me off to Hospice at the end of the week."

"Are you okay with that?"

"What am I gonna do? They say it's pretty nice and the food is better, but I think a couple of the nurses here have a thing for me."

Tom had to admire the fact that Hank retained his sense of humor in spite of everything. He remembered the first time he had met Hank. He was eleven years old and had been pestering his father, Big Tom, to teach him how to fight so he could stand up to the bullies at school. His father, who had long since stopped boxing competitively, still worked out at Southside, finally relented and took Young Tom in to the gym. The whole place smelled of heat and sweat and Tom remembered almost gagging. He and his father walked through the gym and more than a few of the younger fighters nodded to Big Tom almost reverentially.

They walked into a small office in the back where Hank sat behind an old metal desk with a cigarette smoldering in the ashtray. He stood up when they entered.

His father made the introductions, "Tommy this is Mr. Loughran."

Hank held out his hand. Young Tom noticed that the rope-like muscles popping out of the trainer's forearm.

Hank smiled broadly and said, "Little on the small side, but he looks healthy. Maybe make a bantam or a lightweight out of him. Still, should have better footwork than his hulk of a father."

Tom's father had laughed and mussed Tom's hair. Tom smiled but was too nervous to say anything at the time.

"Look kid," Hank said now, pulling Tom back to the present. "The way things look I wasn't sure if I was going to be around much longer and there's been something that's been bothering me."

"What is it?" Tom asked. He had no idea where Hank was going. Hank shifted again and seemed to be thinking. Tom noticed his eyes looked even more glassy than they had before.

"About your dad..." Hank's voice trailed off and he had another coughing fit. Tom waited patiently and looked to see if there was anything nearby for Hank to drink. He picked up a glass of water and offered it to him. Again, Hank waved him off.

"What about him?" Tom asked after Hank's body seemed to calm down.

"I've been keeping this quiet for a long time Tommy. And even now I'm not sure it's the right thing to do."

"Jesus Hank, whatever it is, it sounds like you want to get it off your chest."

Hank closed his eyes and put his head back. He seemed to summon his resolve and then looked back at Tom. "Your dad's death wasn't an accident."

That was it. Tom had always had a suspicion about the "accident" that his father had when Tom was fifteen years old. The official police report, which Tom had seen himself when he was a policeman, had said that Tom Sr. had been extremely intoxicated one night and crashed his car into the Buffalo River at the foot of Vandalia Street. Tom had never known his father to be anything more that a social drinker, let alone reckless enough to drive drunk. He had always had his suspicions; the police report that he had seen was noticeably short on details, but he sometimes wondered if it wasn't just a latent idealization of his late father that wouldn't let him accept the official story.

"What makes you say that Hank?"

Hank swallowed and went on, "The night your dad died he was supposed to be at the gym to help me with a couple of the guys. He was late so I called him on the phone and right away I could tell he was pretty worked up about something. Tommy, me and your pop were pretty tight but it took me a while to get it out of him..."

"Get what out of him?"

"He said he found the guy who killed your sister."

Another blow. Tom's sister Colleen had been killed by a hit and run driver when she was ten years old while she was riding her bike. There had been no eyewitnesses, just a few people who heard a crash and then a car speed off. When they found her she was barely alive and never regained consciousness. Now Hank was saying it was related.

"Who?" was all Tom could utter.

"He only had a last name; 'Mr. Jones' he said. But he claimed to know he had something to do with the Sons of Eire Social Club on Abbott."

"That's it?"

"That's all I could get out of him. I begged him to wait and let me come with him. He said he was headed there now and told me he could take care of himself."

Tom thought about the gun he had found while cleaning out the basement at the family's old house. He wondered if things would have turned out differently if his father had taken it along with him that night. He looked down at Hank who now had tears rolling down his cheeks.

"Tom, I am so sorry," he said weakly. "I should have gone with him."

Tom put his hand on Hank's shoulder and said, "Hey, how the hell were you supposed to know. This all just came out of the blue?"

Hank, recovering his composure somewhat, said, "Yeah, the day before he seemed fine. It's just that, back in the day, the Son's of Eire had a certain air about it."

"What do you mean?"

"I dunno, there were some bad men down there."

Tom thought about Hugh Donovan, his paternal grandfather. Hugh was a bit of a force to be reckoned with himself back in the day, a bar owner and bookmaker among other rumored enterprises.

"Did you ever talk to Hugh about any of this?" he asked.

Hank Loughran grimaced. "A couple of days later I went to the bar to talk to Hugh. He pretty much told me to mind my own business. It was odd though; something was off about the old man."

"What was that?"

"It was the way he said it. You know your granddad; he can be a real prick. But I saw something that day that I'd never seen from him before."

"What do you mean?"

Hank looked at Tom directly and said, "Tommy I survived a year in Korea and a life in the ring with a bunch of guys trying to beat my brains in and there is one thing I can spot in a man's eyes. Hugh was afraid of something."

Tom shook his head. Hugh Donovan was one tough old son of a bitch and he had a hard time thinking that anything could frighten him. Just then Hank closed his eyes and started to cough again, sending his body into convulsions. Tom took Hank's hand and tried to calm him to no avail. After a few minutes two nurses came in and gently pushed Tom out of the way and put an oxygen mask over Hank's mouth and nose.

The older of the two nurses looked up at Tom slightly impatiently and said, "He should really be quiet for a while."

Tom apologized and promised Hank he would come back. As he rode the elevator down to the lobby, he thought about his grandfather and wondered what on earth could have possibly unnerved him enough to react to Hank like that.

He thought about Colleen. Tom was thirteen years old when she died and he realized that as the years passed he had thought about her less and less and that made him feel guilty. He wondered what she would be like if she had gotten a chance at life. Physically, she resembled her mother, olive skin, dark hair and eyes. But where her mother was quiet and retiring Colleen was energetic and could be boisterous and full of piss and vinegar. Her mother's constant urgings to Colleen to be more 'ladylike' had limited effect. While Colleen looked up to Tom, she always did her own thing and fought her own battles. Tom Sr. never seemed to know what to do with his daughter, having been an only child himself and not having an instruction manual for a rambunctious little girl. After she died he seemed more concerned with his wife's near crippling grief than anything. The loss of Colleen would hang heavily over the Donovan home for the next two years.

Tom checked his watch and thought about calling Hugh but then decided to wait until morning. He wanted to be able to look his grandfather in the eye when he asked his questions.

Chapter 3

Tom woke at 6:30 AM and went for a run. The air was crisp and clear without a trace of a breeze. After he showered and shaved he got into his car and drove out to South Buffalo.

The previous week's snow had mostly melted but it had dropped below freezing again and there were still small patches of ice on the sidewalk as he pulled up in front of Donovan's Tavern on South Park Avenue. Donovan's had been built in the shadow of the old Republic Steel Plant and opened up at eight AM for the men just getting off of the third shift. Even though the steel plant and most of the people who kept such hours were a thing of the past, his grandfather, Hugh Donovan had kept the same hours of operation out of some kind of bow to tradition. It was one of the last classic "shot and a beer" places in a neighborhood that used to be dotted with them.

Of course, one of the main reasons the bar had survived as long as it had was that it was a front for Hugh's bookmaking business. However, with the increased availability of state run lotteries as well as other gambling outlets, Hugh's bookmaking business had mostly gone by the wayside. It was rumored though that he still kept up with a few of the side businesses that had sprung up during his life, most of them questionable, but other than the bar and a little sports book he still made, he claimed he was semi-retired.

Tom walked in the front door of the tavern, the smell of stale beer and cigarette smoke thinly covered by the smell of detergent. The television was on over the bar that ran the length of the right hand side of the room. After his eyes adjusted to the dim lighting he realized the room was empty.

A moment later Bonnie, the sixty-something, bottle-blond barmaid came out of the back room carrying a case of beer with a carton of milk balanced on top. She had a cigarette hanging from her mouth and jumped a little when she saw Tom silhouetted in the doorway.

"Jesus Tommy," she said, "You scared the shit out of me."

Tom stepped over and took the beer from Bonnie and let her take the milk. She walked behind the bar and put her cigarette into a tin ashtray on the bar.

Tom followed her behind and placed the beer on the floor by the cooler door and said, "What's a petite flower like yourself doing stocking the bar?"

She chuckled and said, "Kid I've been stocking bars and tossing kegs around since before you were a gleam in your daddy's eyes."

"Where's Whitey?"

She put a stopper in the sink and turned the tap on. She thought for a moment and then said, "He went to pick up your granddad."

"Is Hugh's car in the shop?"

She shook her head. "No, sweetie, Hugh can't drive anymore." She hesitated and then, "When was the last time you talked to him?"

Tom had to think for a moment. After not speaking much in the two years after he lost his job, he and the old man had attempted a bit of a reconciliation. They had grown distant after Tom's father died and then did not speak at all after Tom became a cop. Hugh had reached out to him when Tom found himself in a legal jam the previous spring. Tom had made an effort to get around to see the old man but he found there were things about Hugh that he just couldn't let go.

"It's been a couple of months I guess."

Bonnie smiled sympathetically and said, "I'm not trying to give you a hard time. I know you've been making an effort. Your granddad hasn't been doing too well, health-wise."

Tom wasn't exactly sure but he figured Hugh was probably in his late eighties. He had survived his wife, his son and many of his contemporaries. Given Hugh's colorful life that was no small feat. Even though, he was not immortal, Tom noticed that Hugh was slowing down.

"Is it the diabetes?" he asked.

Bonnie picked up the cigarette and took a drag. "That and all the other stuff that comes with it I guess. Whitey just left. They should be back soon."

Tom didn't want to wait. Hugh's house was only a few blocks away and he would prefer to confront him in front of as few people as possible. He gave Bonnie a hug and she gave him a kiss on the cheek and he left.

A few minutes later he pulled into the driveway behind Whitey Brennan's aged Cadillac and turned off the motor. He knocked on the front door of the Cape Cod style house and Whitey answered it almost immediately. His face lit up when he saw Tom.

"Tommy, you little son of a bitch, get in here," he said putting a beefy hand on Tom's shoulder and pulling him in.

"Good to see you Whitey. Where's the old man?"

Whitey looked over his shoulder at the stairs. "Upstairs, just getting ready." He looked at Tom and his face grew serious. "I don't know if you know it Tom, but the old man has been having a hard time of it lately."

"Yeah, I was just at the bar. Bonnie said he can't drive anymore."

"'Tis true. He hasn't been sleeping much lately either."

Whitey cocked his head to the side and gave Tom a long look. "So, what brings ya here lad?"

Tom knew anything he said to his grandfather he could say to Whitey, who had worked for Hugh since before Tom was born. Tom doubted there was little that went on at Donovan's that Whitey didn't know about. He also felt the residual emotions from his conversation with Hank Loughran coming back.

"I saw Hank Loughran last night."

Tom saw a glimmer of something in Whitey's eye that disappeared just as suddenly.

Whitey looked down and shook his head. "Shame about old Hank," he said. "Hell of a way to go."

"Yeah well, he told me something interesting."

"What would that be?"

Tom thought about Whitey's relationship and closeness to his grandfather and wondered if he knew anything about what he was about to say. Part of him wanted to tell Whitey to cut the crap and come clean with what he knew, but the other part of him wondered if this was a secret Hugh had kept to himself. Everybody had secrets they kept to themselves, usually the worst ones.

"Something I need to ask Hugh about," Tom said.

Whitey grew serious. "I don't know if you should be upsetting him with this Tommy."

"What, that my dad was murdered and it was never properly investigated?"

"Tommy..." Whitey said raising his hands.

"Punch drunk old fool!" A voice came from the top of the stairs. They hadn't heard Hugh come partway down. He looked angry and his fist was shaking. "Why the hell would he stir things up after all these years? And better yet, why would you listen?"

Tom walked over to the foot of the stairs and looked up at Hugh. He could sense Whitey step up beside him.

Tom felt his own anger rise. He wasn't going to be steam- rolled by his grandfather.

"What he said made some sense, and don't forget I had access to the police reports. Something has always been off about this Hugh and you know it."

The old man continued shakily down the stairs until he stood right in front of Tom. He put a finger up in Tom's face and said, "There's nothing there, you little shit. Just the overactive imagination of some brain dead ex-pug."

Tom tried to look into his grandfather's eyes but read only anger coming back at him. He had the briefest sensation that he was looking into a mirror. "I am just as willing to let things lie as the next guy, but I think there's something you're not telling me."

"Bullshit!" Hugh sputtered. "First off, you are as stubborn as an old Dago washer woman. I blame your mother's side for that. Secondly, it is what it is and you should just let it go."

Tom stepped back and shook his head.

Hugh went on, "For Christ's sake Tom, it's been over twenty years. Let it go. I got nothing to tell you that would make anything different."

With that Hugh started to waver and Whitey stepped forward to steady him. Tom was frustrated and annoyed but he felt bad for having pushed the old man's buttons. Whitey eased Hugh over to a chair and then shot Tom a dirty look. Tom realized he wouldn't be getting anything out of the old man and saying anything else would be regrettable so he turned and went quietly out the front door.

Chapter 4

It wasn't until Tom was older that he understood what little he knew about what his father did while he was alive. For as long as he could recall, his father had been a part of the local laborers' union. What he did for them was never really clear, some kind of union official or other. What Tom did remember was his father often being out late or keeping odd hours when he was "doing something for grandpa Hugh."

Tom hadn't been totally naive. His grandfather had been kind of a neighborhood legend back in the day, not so much to himself or his peers, but to their parents and grandparents. But the kids whispered things at school; sometimes it kept him out of trouble, sometimes the opposite, with some young thug trying to show he wasn't afraid of any of the Donovans. Tom had learned how to fight and stand up for himself.

All these things came back to Tom as he pondered his grandfather's involvement in his father's death. It frustrated him that the old man wasn't giving anything up easily, either a denial, or a confession, or even a claim of ignorance for that matter. He drove from the South side through downtown to the office at Frederickson and Associates. He realized he had become so lost in thought that he had made the trip more or less on mental autopilot and had arrived at the office on Delaware Avenue.

Frederickson and Associates took up half of the first floor of a solid brick building that had been built in the 1930's. It had originally been an apartment building, but as Buffalo boomed in the 30's and 40's and downtown expanded, so did the need for office space. At one time, it had been a dentist's office and then housed a law firm. Cal Fredrickson had occupied the space for the past eight years, adding some modifications but leaving the building's original heavy wood trim and other details. The office was wired like any other modern space but its overall appearance looked like something from a bygone era.

He sat in his car for a moment, considering whether or not to go in. He currently had no active assignment, but had to put the finishing touches on some paperwork from his last job. He thought about the dead end he was at with the questions he had regarding his father and then thought of a way forward.

The agency employed an "IT" man by the name of Brian Dinkle. The title was misleading, as Brian's main job at the agency was research and fact checking. Most of it was legitimate, but Brian was also good at finding things hidden beyond what would be considered public record, all of it done with Cal Frederickson's unspoken approval.

Tom entered the reception area and was relieved to see Cal's door closed. In front of his door sat Cal's second wife and administrative assistant, Grace. When she looked up at Tom he detected a bit of distress behind her clear blue eyes and then immediately figured out the cause. Cal's voice boomed from his inner office. It was hardly the first time anyone at the office had heard Cal raise his voice, but it was always better to be on the other side of his door when it happened.

Tom pointed his chin at the door and raised his eyebrows. "Who?" he asked quietly.

"Gil," she whispered back.

Gil Adams was another retired cop. He had been with the Erie County Sheriff's office for twenty years and had gotten to know Cal when Cal was a detective with the Buffalo PD. He and another retiree, Simon Willis, worked part-time for Cal and shared an office at the opposite end of the suite from Tom and Sherry.

Tom nodded and started to turn towards the hallway and Brian's office but Grace stopped him.

"Tom, don't go anywhere," she said gesturing over her shoulder to her husband's office. "He's going to want to see you."

Crap, Tom thought. He was hoping to take a few days and work on his own thing. He found Brian Dinkle in his office loading one of his laptops into a bag. It looked like he was getting ready to leave.

"Hey, Tommy boy. Did you come to say goodbye?"

Uh oh, Tom thought. "Where are you off to Bri'?"

"Tampa Bay, Spring Computer Con."

"Sounds exciting. When are you leaving?"

Brian checked the time on his smart phone. Tom felt old suddenly because he noticed his might be the last generation to wear a wristwatch. "Catching a plane in about twelve hours."

"How long will you be gone for?"

"About a week." Brian looked at Tom and furrowed his brow. "Is there something you need?"

Tom smiled wanly. "Well, now that you mention it-"

"Tommy, I've got a list of things to do before I get on that plane."

"This should just take an hour or two."

Brian looked at him for a moment. "Would this research be of the sensitive variety?" he asked.

"Could be, depending on where it takes you," Tom said as he pulled his notebook out of his coat pocket.

Brian held out his hand and stepped towards Tom. "Alright, I'll do what I can, but if it's all the same I think I will do it from home. Cal's been getting a little antsy lately about some of my research."

"I appreciate it Brian." He tore out the page of questions and names he wanted Brian to look into and handed it over.

Brian took the sheet and started to skim it. "And I suppose this can't wait until I get back..." A flicker of recognition came over him and he looked up. "Jesus Tom, is this about your dad?"

Tom felt himself blush slightly. "Yeah, just a couple of nagging questions I need to have answered."

Brian thought for a moment and then said, "Well all the more reason to do this from home if it's not agency business." He put the paper in his laptop bag and considered Tom again. "Just out of curiosity, why now, after all this time?"

"An old family friend told me something last night that kind of made me start to wonder..." Tom's voice trailed off.

"Ah, I see. New shit has come to light."

"Excuse me?"

"Sorry," Brian said. "It's a line from '*The Big Lebowski*'."

"Never saw it."

"Seriously? Do yourself a favor. It's a classic."

"I'll take your word for it."

Tom thanked Brian and Brian said not to thank him until he actually found something for him given the age of the incident and his tight schedule. They said goodbye and Tom almost collided with Cal Frederickson as he left Brian's office. To Tom's relief it looked like Cal had calmed down somewhat.

"You're clear on the Puccio thing?" Cal asked, referring to Tom's most recent assignment.

"Uh... yeah. I just have a little paper work to do."

"It's going to have to wait. Come with me." With that Cal turned around and headed back down the hall before Tom could protest.

They were seated in Cal's office and Cal pushed a file folder across his desk towards Tom. "I need you to take this over from Adams."

"What is it?"

"We've been hired by an insurance company to find out if the man in that file, a Mr. Roger Wozniak, is indeed injured as he's claiming, or if he is trying to scam his employer and our client. Rumor has it he has been doing some construction work with his brother and getting paid off the books while he's collecting disability."

Tom opened the folder and found the overview of the case on top. Wozniak worked for a freight company and had claimed he had been injured when the lift gate on a truck he was unloading malfunctioned causing him to fall off and injure his back. No one had witnessed the incident and Wozniak had been in and out of trouble with his employer before. Tom flipped through the next few pages, some information that obviously had been collected by Brian Dinkle, and stopped when he got to a copy of Wozniak's injury claim. Most of it was fairly plain but Tom asked, "What is 'loss of consortium'?"

"It means he can't get it on with his girlfriend," Cal responded without a trace of a smile.

Tom nodded and looked back at the file. He was trying to think of a way to get out of it.

"And what happened with Gil Adams?"

Cal frowned. "Our esteemed colleague was made by Mr. Wozniak."

"Was he sure he was made?"

Cal was getting agitated and Tom now regretted pushing him. Cal sat forward in his chair and said, "Well he was confronted by Mr. Wozniak on the street in front of his residence, so yes, I would say he was made. Then, to make matters worse, when the police arrived Gil thought it would be prudent to show his PBA card and identify himself. The Kenmore police were hardly impressed and threatened to charge him with harassment if he did not make himself scarce. So, our friend, Gil, came back to the office with his tail between his legs and here we are." As he finished he spread his hands.

Tom loathed surveillance work. It was tedious and often fruitless. Now, because of what Gil Adams had done, it would also be more difficult, with the subject aware that he was being watched.

He really wanted to keep going on his father's case but didn't know how to explain it to Cal without sounding crazy.

Cal interrupted his thoughts; "As you know, Ms. Palkowski will be leaving us in a couple of weeks. I want you two to split this and if we don't have anything by then we will evaluate the merits of continuing surveillance of Mr. Wozniak at that time." Cal looked hard at Tom. "Something on your mind, son?"

Tom hadn't realized he must have looked irritated. "No," he said, checking his watch. "It's late afternoon now. I take it you want us to pick up Wozniak in the morning?"

Cal seemed slightly placated. "That sounds fine." He looked down at another file he had on his desk officially ending the meeting.

Tom realized he still had several hours of daylight left, so he decided to do a short reconnaissance on Roger Wozniak. On his way out to the car, he left a message for Sherry to call him back so they could figure out a schedule.

He really hoped that he wouldn't be stuck spying on Wozniak for three or four weeks. He had questions that had gone from being a mild buzz in the back of his mind to a raging alarm that needed to be answered. A lot of it depended on what Brian would be able to find out for him. Brian was a pretty proficient researcher, but he was eccentric, even on his best days. Given that he was off to Florida to spend a week with his ilk, Tom wondered how much attention his project would get.

Donovan had been with the agency for over a year and a half and had learned to adjust to the ups and downs that came with being a PI. The job could be a grind, but it was probably the closest thing to police work he was going to see if he stayed in the area. Insurance cases, however, he still did not enjoy. There was no love lost for the insurance companies, who always seemed to be trying to get out of paying people. At the same time he didn't care for somebody trying to scam the system. The whole process could be pretty sordid.

He found Roger Wozniak's house just as the sun was setting. It was a modest two story 1950's era house on Tremont Avenue, a block and a half off of Military Road. He did a moderately slow drive by and saw an older pick-up truck with a toolbox in the bed and a newer Ford compact parked in front of it. From the file he had on Wozniak, Tom knew that the truck belonged to Wozniak and the car to his live-in girlfriend. He also learned that Wozniak was divorced and had two children who lived with his ex-wife in nearby Tonawanda. There was alternating one side of the street parking, which was good. You could try to blend in with the other cars on the street and move occasionally to avoid unwanted attention, (a method that was obviously lost on Gil Adams). The only question was how many cars would still be parked on the street during the course of a normal workday.

Tom blew out a deep breath and turned for home.

Chapter 5

The next day was Wednesday and Tom had camped out down the street from Roger Wozniak's house just after sunrise. If Wozniak was doing construction work with his brother, then the chances were they would be at it early in the morning when contractors generally started, and Tom didn't want to miss Wozniak if he left early.

Nothing happened until shortly after eight-thirty when Wozniak left his house and Tom followed him at a safe distance to a medical office on Sheridan Drive. Again, Tom found himself wondering just how fruitless this whole endeavor would be. Wozniak had to know he was being watched and would have to be an idiot to do anything to derail his lawsuit. Tom and Sherry could be as stealthy as humanly possible and it could all be in vain.

Sherry called while he was waiting in the parking lot for Wozniak to reemerge. They arranged for Sherry to relieve Tom after the visit to the doctor's office. He tailed Wozniak until he turned off of Elmwood on to Tremont. He called

Sherry to make sure she was in place and then peeled off.

He thought about going back to his apartment but decided to head over to his mother's home in North Buffalo to kill a few hours. It was closer and he could see if she needed help with anything around the house. He wouldn't say anything to her about his father just yet. After twenty-three years she barely spoke about her husband's death. Actually, she had become withdrawn after it. She was had still grieving over the loss of Tom's sister Colleen, and then Big Tom died. Tom barely saw the bright, loving woman he had known after that. She had been a good mother to him, but there was damage and an emptiness that could not be repaired.

And Brian. He still hadn't heard from Brian Dinkle and had assumed that his travel itinerary had prevented him from doing any serious research. He had just started to curse Brian's name when his phone buzzed. He fished it out of his coat pocket and answered it.

"Major Tom?" It was Brian.

"Brian, I was just thinking about you."

Tom heard a PA announcement in the background and knew Brian was in an airport.

"Where are you?" Tom asked.

"Baltimore, one hour lay-over. And I'm flattered that you miss me already."

Tom immediately pulled over and took out his notebook. "Did you find anything?" he asked.

"Yup, couple 'a things..."

Tom waited. He could hear the faint sounds of Brain typing something onto his keyboard.

"First off, as you know, no one from the Buffalo PD signed off on the final report of your father's accident."

"Yeah, I saw that a few years back when I did a little digging."

"Well, I went back a little farther and found some other paperwork on the investigation and there was one cop's name that came up more than a few times."

"Who was that?" Tom asked. He had only seen the final report.

"Detective Bernard Kennedy. That ring a bell?"

"Never heard of him."

"Guess you wouldn't have. He retired in '95."

"Shit. Is he even still alive?"

"According to city records, he is. His pension check is mailed down to an address in Punta Gorda, Florida."

Shit, Tom thought. How am I going to get a hold of him? Then he asked, "What about this Mr. Jones that Hank mentioned?"

"No luck there. I tried to tie him in with the Sons of Eire Social Club and came up empty. They don't have a membership roster on line and that is not exactly the most unusual name to do a search on."

Tom looked down at the few lines he had written and thought for a moment. "Okay, thanks Brian. That gives me somewhere to start."

"Wish I could have done more bro'."

"Hey, I didn't expect much of anything after all these years."

"This really bothers you, doesn't it?" Brian asked.

"What's that?"

Brian hesitated and then said, "I could see where you might think there was something fishy going on. I've looked at a lot of police reports and this one looks like it was deliberately left void of information."

That was something Tom had wondered about himself, but no one else had ever said it out loud. He found his emotions mixed, relieved that another person thought that something may have been covered up, and angry that it had been covered up in the first place. He heard another PA announcement in the background and it snapped him back into the present.

"Hey, Tom. They're calling my flight." Brian said.

"Yeah, thanks again Bri'. I owe you one."

"Don't worry about it. You know I am going to be hooking up with some friends of mine at this expo, some pretty resourceful people actually."

Tom didn't know where this was headed. "Okay..."

"I was thinking if we pool our resources maybe we could dig a little deeper."

"Brian, I appreciate it but I don't want anybody to get in trouble."

Brian laughed and said, "Tommy, the people I am talking about live for this shit."

They said goodbye and rang off. Tom started his car and resumed the drive towards his mother's house. He couldn't stop thinking about Detective Bernard Kennedy; why had his name been left off the final report? Was it just a clerical error or was there something else. And the elusive

Mr. Jones, the man his father was going to meet with on the night that he died; was he a dead end?

Chapter 6

Tom and Sherry spent the better part of Thursday and Friday basically watching Roger Wozniak do nothing. The time spent was increasingly tedious and Tom was almost certain Wozniak's encounter with Gil Adams had scared him off of doing anything foolish. On Saturday Sherry had the first watch and she called Tom at 9:00 AM to say that Wozniak's ex-wife had dropped his kids off. They decided to discontinue their surveillance until Monday.

Early Monday morning, Tom was sitting in his car freezing his ass off. The temperature had dropped into the twenties and there was a stiff wind coming from the West. Again there was no sign of movement from Wozniak's house. Tom had finished a large coffee and was thinking about running around the corner to grab another one and use the restroom when his phone buzzed on the seat next to him. He caught it on the second ring.

"Tommy boy!" It was Brian Dinkle.

"Hey Brian. You're not back in town are you?"

"Hell no. This thing is raging on all week and I intend to stay to the bitter end."

Tom checked his watch; it was 8:10 AM. "You getting an early start?" he asked.

"No my friend, actually just about to turn in."

"Aren't you going to miss the expo?"

Brian chuckled. "Yeah, the boring ass part. No Tommy, the real expo happens at night. That's when my like-minded brethren get together and find out what's really going on."

Tom thought about what it would be like to be in a room full of Brian Dinkles and shook his head. "Sounds interesting," he said.

"Oh it can be," Brian replied. "Remember the people I said might be able to help me with our research?"

"Yeah."

"Well, my friend, Tuna, showed me a little back door into a certain government agency's archives and I came up with a couple of things you may be interested in."

At first Tom had been wondering what kind of person went with the name 'Tuna,' but then

Brian's claim made him sit up. "What's that?" he asked.

"Well, I don't have a positive ID on your Mr. Jones but I think we may have found a thread that could be looked into."

Tom was dumbfounded. He had thought that Mr. Jones was a dead end. "What did you find?"

"Did you know," Brian began, "that in the mid-to late-eighties the Son's of Eire Social Club was under FBI surveillance?"

"For what?"

"It looks like the club had some kind of connection to the Irish Republican Army."

"What?"

"I know, sounds crazy right? Here we all thought they just held parades and step-danced."

Tom took out his notebook and turned to a fresh page. "And Mr. Jones?"

"Well, that's the thing that kind of ties it all together. None of the IRA guys back in the day used their real names. Any communication they had was made using aliases; Mr. Smith, Mr. Jones."

Tom thought for a second and said, "And there was mention of Mr. Jones?"

"You got it. The name came up at least a half dozen times in connection with the Sons of Eire from 1985 to 1989. Not only were they watching out for IRA soldiers, but they also thought that there were people sympathetic to the cause raising money in Buffalo."

"Seriously?" Tom asked. A woman who looked vaguely familiar passed by his car walking a small dog.

"Seriously. Have you ever heard of such shenanigans?"

Tom turned his attention back to Brian. "No," he said. "Even when I was on the job. It must have been pretty hush-hush on both ends."

"Both ends?" Brian asked.

"Yeah, the club and the Feds."

Out of the corner of his eye Tom noticed the woman with the dog stop with her back to the front of his car.

"I thought it might be a stretch," Brian was saying. "But it would be quite the coincidence wouldn't it. Tom, are you still there?"

"Shit," Tom replied. The woman turned around and he realized it was Roger Wozniak's live-in girlfriend and she had a phone in her hand. Tom was pretty sure she was taking a picture of his license plate. He put his head down and pretended not to see her. She shot him a dirty look and turned back towards her house.

"Shit, Brian I have to go."

"Oh... okay. That's about all we had so far anyway."

"Thanks, man. I mean it. Look, I don't want you to spend your whole trip running this stuff down." Tom had started his car and pulled away from the curb.

"No worries Major Tom. Like I said we enjoy this stuff. It's educational and fun."

And probably a felony Tom thought. "Again, I do appreciate it," he said.

"You're welcome."

They rang off and Tom slowly turned the corner onto Military Road and punched in Sherry's number. She picked it up on the fourth ring.

"Hey," she said breathlessly.

"Sher' I got a problem. Where are you?"

"At the gym. I was just about to break a land-speed record on the treadmill. What's up?"

"I think I've been made."

"Shit. By Wozniak?"

"No, the girlfriend. She took my picture and everything."

It sounded like Sherry let out a snort and suddenly Tom felt embarrassed. He had done exactly what Gil Adams had done to get him into this in the first place.

She seemed to recover her composure and said, "I can be there in twenty minutes. Any sign of him moving?"

"No not yet. Listen, give me a call when you get here will you?"

"Sure," she said and disconnected.

>>><<<

Twenty-five minutes later, Tom arrived at his apartment and was getting out of his car when Sherry called him and said she was in place down the street from Wozniak's home. Tom thought, to her credit, she didn't break his balls about blowing the surveillance and told him they would figure something out.

After checking to make sure that his downstairs neighbor wasn't home, he went into the spare room to work out his frustration on the speed bag he had mounted there. He got a good rhythm going on the bag and then put a little extra into it, helping him remove some of the stress from his shoulders.

He knew he was going to have to tell Cal Frederickson that he had been compromised before the end of the day, but he needed to clear his head first and figure out the best way to approach it. He finally decided that the direct approach would be the best, as Cal didn't suffer excuses.

After a half-hour on the bag he took a shower and checked his phone and saw he hadn't received any calls or messages. He went into the dining room to boot up his laptop. He had been thinking about what Brian had told him about 'Mr. Jones' so he did his own search on the Sons of Eire Social Club. He knew he would never find anything that Brian hadn't or wouldn't find but he wanted to get a feel for the place.

The club had been established in 1902 by a fresh wave of Irish immigrants to the Buffalo area. They were looking to organize themselves politically and socially as they tried to gain some traction against the other immigrants who had come before them.

Apparently they had drawn the ire of the notorious newspaper owner and labor boss William "Fingy" Connors and their original Clubhouse was burned down under suspicious circumstances. The Club went underground for a few years and then resurfaced keeping a lower profile, acting more as a social center and meeting place. It had moved two more times over the years, finally settling in its current location on Abbott Road in the city's South side.

Since the fire at the start of the last century Tom couldn't seem to find another mention of the Club being involved in any kind of politics, either local or international. The closest thing was a blurb he found from the 70's that said that families were being sought to house children from Belfast for the summer as part of a relief effort for the strife torn city. The agency running the effort was well known and had an impeccable reputation, so that looked like a dead end.

The Club's own web site was also devoid of anything incriminating, or interesting for that matter, information. Basically, it contained a brief (if sanitized) history, a list of current officers and community events. There was no membership roster or information on past members.

Tom checked his watch; it was shortly after three. He turned off his computer and grabbed his jacket. He would have to tell Cal face- to-face what had happened. It would have looked pretty pathetic to try to do it over the phone. He punched in Sherry's number to tell her he was on his way to the office.

"Hi, Mom," Sherry said when she answered. Tom heard a man's voice in the background.

"What's up?" Tom asked quietly, knowing she probably couldn't talk.

"Had a little car trouble... hang on," she said. Tom heard her talking to someone else and then she came back. "I'll be there in a half hour, gotta go." And she ended the call.

Tom was momentarily concerned. But then Sherry hadn't sounded distressed and if she was in any kind of a situation she probably wouldn't have answered her phone. He scrapped the idea of going to the office and instead started to head over towards Kenmore to see if she needed help. He had just about reached his front door when his phone buzzed and he answered it immediately.

"Where are you?" Sherry asked.

"I'm home. Are you alright?"

"Never better," she said. If you could actually hear somebody smile over the phone, this was one of those times, Tom thought.

"Sherry, what are you doing?"

"Never mind that, Donovan. Did you talk to Cal yet?"

"No, I was just on my way in to tell him."

"Well, don't. Not yet anyway."

"Sherry, what's going on?" Tom asked a little impatiently.

She was almost giddy now. "It's hard to explain. Check your email and call me back." She rang off again.

Tom turned on his laptop again and logged on to his email account. There was a new message from Sherry's cell phone with a video file attached. Tom opened the file and the video started.

Tom shook his head as he watched the image of Roger Wozniak changing a tire on Sherry's Toyota, all the time keeping up a running dialog with her. He seemed oblivious to the fact that he was being recorded, actually more interested in hitting on Sherry. As he was finishing up her phone buzzed, Tom knew that it was probably his call to Sherry, and the video cut out. A moment later it had come back on and Wozniak seemed to be making a final attempt. Sherry must have been holding the phone at her side, because the shot of Wozniak was from a low angle. Still it was undeniably him talking.

"I can't believe your boyfriend would let you drive around on a tire with a hole in it," Wozniak said.

"He can be a real jerk sometimes, but what are you going to do, you know?" Sherry replied.

Wozniak shook his head. "A girl like you? You probably have more options than you could shake a stick at."

Tom heard Sherry giggle, which was highly uncharacteristic, and say, "I don't know. We've been together a long time; we're a good fit."

"Well, maybe somebody a little older," Wozniak said raising his eyebrows. "A guy who's been around and knows how to take care of a woman and her car."

Dude, give it up, Tom thought.

"You're sweet," Sherry said. "And quite the gentleman, I'm sure your wife appreciates you."

Wozniak smiled again. "I'm divorced actually, got married too young. But hey, I do know how to please a lady."

Sherry giggled again and handed Wozniak a slip of paper. "Well thanks again Roger. Maybe we could have coffee sometime."

"Or drinks," Wozniak replied looking down at the paper. He started to back away to his truck and said, "You take care of yourself Brittney." The screen went blank.

"What did you do?" Tom asked Sherry when she answered her phone.

"Look, there was probably no way we were going to catch ol' Roger doing something stupid unless we dangled a carrot. I just appealed to his sense of chivalry."

"I don't know Sher'. That kind of thing never holds up in court."

"Well, time is of the essence Donovan. After this morning this is as close as we were probably going to get. Besides, how often do these things go to trial anyway? We give our client some leverage, as well as proof that Wozniak is far from disabled."

Tom thought for a moment and then said. "He did make quite the production of it while he was fixing your tire."

Sherry chuckled. "Yeah and he didn't even mention his 'loss of consortium.' Actually he seemed to suggest he was quite capable of consortium."

Tom smiled in spite of himself. "Are you still watching him?"

"Hell no," she said. "You and I are going to go to Cal and show him my home movie. Wozniak has seen half the agency up close and personal and we all have better things to do."

"He's not going to like it," Tom said.

"I know Tom, but this is the best I think we can do. Besides, I have less than two weeks left. What's he going to do, fire me?"

Chapter 7

When they arrived at the office, Sherry explained to Cal that she had a video that would probably get Roger Wozniak to drop his claim against his employer and their insurance company. At first, Cal seemed incredulous, but he had Sherry email him the video and opened it up on his desktop computer.

Cal's office was deathly quiet except for the sound coming from the video. Tom and Sherry were seated in front of his desk, feeling like a couple of kids in the principal's office, watching Cal's brow become more furrowed as the video played. The video ended and Cal exhaled audibly and looked at them.

"Whose idea was this?" he said, pointing at the computer.

"Mine," Sherry said.

Cal focused on Tom and said, "And you thought this was a good idea?"

Tom wasn't about to throw Sherry under the bus. "Sherry took a chance because I got made this morning," he said.

"Say what now?"

"Wozniak's girlfriend made me, I'm pretty sure. I peeled off and called Sherry and she-"

Cal put a beefy index finger up stopping Tom. "So you knew about this?"

Tom could feel his face getting hot.

"Only after the fact," Sherry threw in. Fortunately, Tom thought, she had dropped the bemused look she had had before.

Cal looked directly at her and spread his hands to prompt an explanation.

"I know I took a chance, but technically this isn't entrapment because Wozniak didn't do anything illegal. He just showed he's capable of doing physical labor as well as suggested there has been no disruption in his libido."

Tom didn't know whether to laugh or cringe at that, so he looked at Cal to see how it went over. Cal was looking down at his desk blotter writing something down and Tom thought he saw the smallest trace of a smile.

"Besides," Sherry continued, "How many times do these things even go to trial? Odds are Wozniak put his side jobs on hold until he got paid so what have we lost?"

Cal's face became stern again. "Still, it was damned reckless. And if it ever did go to trial this would be thrown right out for numerous reasons. I am going to send it to our client with an apology and try to think of a good way to say that 'this is all you are going to get from us.' Now, Donovan, if you will excuse us, I need to speak to Ms. Palkowski for a moment."

"Cal—" Tom started.

"Out," Cal said pointing towards the door.

Tom looked over at Sherry, who looked like she didn't have a care in the world and figured she could take care of herself. He excused himself and went down the hall to his office.

It was just before 5:00 PM and Tom suddenly realized his schedule was wide open. He left a note on Sherry's desk to call him and went out the door.

>>><<<

Two hours later he pulled up to the curb across the street from the Sons of Eire Social Club. It was a two story commercial building with a brick facade and a double glass door entrance two steps up off the sidewalk. The vestibule looked dark. It didn't look like anybody was there. Tom pulled back out and looked into the lot next to the building; there were two cars parked towards the back of the lot. He pulled in and got out, the cold sleet stinging his face, and walked around to the front of the building.

He climbed the steps and pulled on the right side door. To his surprise it opened. He stepped into the vestibule and let his eyes adjust to the dark. To his right, a glass door with an ascending staircase on the other side of it was marked "private." To his left, the sign on the glass door said "Sons of Eire Social Club." He went through that one.

The interior looked like just about any other South Buffalo tavern Tom had ever seen. The walls were paneled and there were pictures and a few posters on the wall. The bar ran along most of right side of the room. There was a slight guy with pale skin and dark hair behind the bar. It looked like he was bleeding a beer tap. There was another person in the room; at one of the heavy wooden tables sat a heavyset man with red hair turning to gray, tuning a guitar. The guitar player seemed to do a double take and then stared at Tom for a moment. This must have got the barman's attention because he stopped what he was doing and called out to Tom.

"Are ye here for darts then?" He asked with a slight Irish brogue. "League doesn't start 'til eight o'clock."

Tom broke off his stare with the guitar player and smiled at the bartender. "No, actually, I just had a couple of questions about the club."

Tom realized then he hadn't prepared at all for his approach to the Sons of Eire. The bartender looked to be in his late twenties, too young to have been around in 1989. But, at the same time, when he heard the word 'questions' he had adopted a defensive pose, placing his arms across his chest.

Tom walked up to the bar and out of his peripheral vision he saw that the guitar player had abandoned his table and left the bar through a door at the back of the room. The bar man looked at him expectantly but wasn't giving anything away.

"I guess my main question is are you accepting new members?"

That seemed to put the bartender at ease a bit. "I believe we are," he said.

Tom offered his hand over the bar. "My name is Tom Boyle," he said.

The bartender actually smiled and shook Tom's hand, "I'm Dominic."

"Nice to meet you Dominic. Are you a member?"

"No, I just man the bar five nights a week."

"Oh, have you been working here long?"

"A bit less than a year, I think. Well, you met the first requirement for membership. Would ya like something to drink?"

"What requirement is that?" Tom asked, studying the beer taps.

"A name like Boyle it would tell me that you are of Irish ancestry."

Tom took a ten-dollar bill out of his wallet. "I am. Not as directly as you, I guess, but a few generations anyway. I'll have a pint of Harp."

Dominic stepped over to the tap to draw a pint. "The other requirement is usually being sponsored by an active member."

Tom racked his brain to try to remember if he knew anyone associated with the club. He let his eyes wander as he thought and then he saw it; to the left of the bar was a picture of a much younger Hank Loughran in his boxing gear, in a fighter's stance with an intense look in his eye. Hank had retired long before Tom had been born, but Tom recognized the picture as a copy of one from Hank's office. Dominic set the fresh pint down on a coaster in front of Tom.

Tom pointed in the direction of the photo and took a chance. "I'm close personal friends with that guy," he said.

Dominic looked at the photo and then said, "Ah, ol' Hank. I'm not sure if he's an active member, but from what I understand he's a bit of a local legend."

"That he is," Tom said smiling.

"Haven't seen the old fella in a while. I understand he's not well."

"He's up at Roswell Park as a matter of fact. Doesn't look too good."

"That's a shame..." Dominic's voice trailed off. Another man had emerged from the door that the guitar player had disappeared through. Tom glanced over and saw a heavy set man with steel gray hair and a ruddy complexion looking back at him through a cloud of smoke from the cigarette hanging from his lips. There must have been a gesture made that Tom hadn't seen because the next words out of Dominic's mouth were, "I'll be right back."

Dominic left the room on the heels of the other man and was gone for a few minutes. When he came back, he took his place behind the bar and

had a look on his face like he had just gotten h
is ass handed to him.

"I'm afraid I was mistaken, Mr. Boyle. The
Club isn't accepting new members at this time."

The thought crossed Tom's mind that he
should ask Dominic who the guy was who had just
put the brakes on his becoming a member, but the
pained expression on the bartender's face told him
that it would probably go nowhere. He left a couple
of dollars on the bar and said, "That's too bad.
Well, thanks anyway."

He couldn't help but notice the look of relief
on Dominic's face. That reaffirmed what he
already thought, that the guy was just a bartender,
not part of a criminal conspiracy.

The wind had died down and it didn't feel
as cold when Tom left the way he came. The sun
had mostly gone down and the streetlights had all
come on. He went around to the side of the
building and was just about to get in his car when
he saw the gray haired man from the bar smoking
another cigarette by the service entrance towards
the back of the building. He could tell the man was
watching him through half closed lids.

They stood and stared at each other for a
moment. Tom knew he should let it go, but was
curious to see what would happen if he gave the

guy a little push. He walked over to about five feet from where the man was standing.

"So you're not taking new members?" he asked.

The man squinted harder and said, "That's right."

"So you're like what, some kind of club officer?"

"Something like that."

Tom held the man's stare. "And your name is?"

The man took a long drag on the cigarette. "Fuck off, junior," he said as he exhaled.

"Well now, Mr. Fuck Off Junior, that's not a very sociable manner for an officer of a social club."

The man took a step forward glaring at Tom. "Well, let me explain it to you then," he said. "Just because you know that punch drunk old fuck doesn't mean shit to me. Also, your name's not really Boyle is it? Probably not even Irish are you?"

"You got me there Mr. Fuck Off. I'm half Italian on my mother's side."

The man smirked and said, "Well, there you have it. We're a private club so we wouldn't have to admit the spawn of some Dago whore if we didn't

72

want to." As he finished, he flicked his cigarette butt at Tom's feet.

Nice, Tom thought, go right to the 'your mama's a whore' card.

Tom took another step forward and the two men were only a few feet apart. "Well that's good to know," he said. "Probably for the better. I grew up around here and I have never met a sorrier lot than the people who've lived in South Buffalo for generations and still claim to be Irish. They all like to talk a good game and act all tough, but when it's all said and done, they are just a bunch of loud-mouthed, drunken, wife-beating, low rent motherfuckers."

He had the man's full attention now. He was balling his fist and staring even harder at Tom.

Tom continued like he just had another thought; "Oh, that's right, you guys are different. With your secret society, with your bombs and your rebel songs. Still talk about fighting a war that you're safely removed from while you sit here on your fat ass—"

The man had heard enough, he spun on the balls of his feet and threw a punch at Tom's head. Tom was ready and he ducked under the blow easily. The man wasn't done. He lunged at Tom and threw a left hand towards Tom's midsection. Tom spun slightly and absorbed the blow with his elbow. It still hurt, the guy was throwing haymakers and putting all his weight into his punches. Tom straightened up as the man threw a wild right hook towards his head. He dodged that and grabbed the man by the shoulder and used his momentum to push him face first into the side of the building.

As the man spun around, he was surprised to see Tom right behind him and even more surprised when Tom hit him in the eye with a left jab. The man let himself bounce off the wall and was raising his fists when Tom's right hand caught him full on underneath his jaw. He fell in a heap at Tom's feet.

The man, conscious but mumbling incoherently, rolled over onto his side. Tom flexed his fingers and, satisfied nothing was broken said, "I learned that from the punch drunk old fuck." He went to his car and climbed in.

He didn't think that anyone had seen the altercation but he wasn't going to hang around and find out. A thought occurred to him, Hank Loughran seemed to be pretty well known at the Sons of Eire, something he had never mentioned. Was there something that Hank had held back the other night? As he pulled out of the lot he saw the man in his rear view mirror trying to get to his feet. He would have to take a run at Hank and find another angle.

Chapter 8

Tom figured that there was about a half an hour of visiting time left after he parked his car in the parking ramp and entered the front doors at Roswell. The last thing he wanted to do was cause Hank any grief, but he had the feeling that he may have been holding something back on him. After seeing that Hank was somewhat of a celebrity at the Sons of Eire, as well as Hank's cryptically mentioning a certain element present at the club in the late eighties, Tom had to be sure.

After getting a visitor's pass from a frowning, white haired volunteer in the lobby he rode the elevator up to the fifth floor. He was trying to think of the best way to broach the subject when he entered the room and was surprised to see that Hank wasn't there. There was an orderly making the bed up who looked up when Tom entered.

"Where's Mr. Loughran?" Tom asked after he rechecked the door to make sure he was in the right room.

The orderly shrugged. "I dunno, I just got to this floor. You can check with the nurse."

Tom went back down the hall to the nurse's station to find it deserted. He looked down to the other end and saw two nurses entering another room. He leaned as far over the counter as he could to see if there was any paperwork with Hank's name on it.

"Can I help you?" came a voice from behind him. Tom turned around to face a young Asian woman with the name Dr. Chu embroidered on her white coat.

"Yes Doctor," he said. "I'm a friend of Hank Loughran's. He was in room 517 but he's not there right now."

Dr. Chu's expression turned slightly sad. "Oh, yes. I'm sorry to tell you that Mr. Loughran passed away late this afternoon." She looked genuinely sympathetic.

Tom was stunned. He forgot all about his reason for being there as the realization that he would never see his boyhood mentor again washed over him.

"I didn't realize he was that close..." his voice trailed off.

"Well, it happens sometimes. We had actually had him set up with a bed at Hospice at the end of this week. Your friend was very ill and we had stopped treatment. But he was a tough old guy and we didn't expect it that soon either." For the first time, her delivery slipped into a slight accent.

"He just died?"

"It happens. His organs were wracked with the disease and were shutting down. After a while the heart just can't keep up. He just stopped breathing." She paused to see if Tom had any questions. When he just looked down at the floor she said, "As sick as he was, your friend was still full of life. He seemed like a very nice man."

"He was," Tom said looking back up at her attempting to smile. "Do you know if anyone claimed the body?"

Dr. Chu shook her head. "According to his chart, he donated his remains to the research center."

Made sense, Tom thought. Hank had been married and divorced once, and had no children. As far as Tom knew, he had no other family. Just like Hank, still trying to teach people things even after he was gone.

Dr. Chu lingered for a moment and then excused herself to resume her rounds. Tom thanked her and headed back to the elevator.

On the way down to the lobby, he noticed that there was something gnawing at the back of his mind. Part of him told himself that he was being paranoid but then again he had the feeling that this was one of those times that the worst kind of question was the one that went unasked. As the elevator descended the feeling got stronger.

What if Hank had had help leaving this world? Given what he had told Tom the other night and the reaction of the people Tom had questioned about it so far, was it totally out of the question? The elevator opened up and he made his way to the information desk.

The woman who had issued his pass was on the phone and Tom handed the plastic card to the other white-haired lady seated next to her. The name badge on her sweater said 'Helen.'

"Helen," Tom said, "I was wondering if you could do me a favor?"

Helen looked up at him and smiled. "What would that be?"

"I was wondering if I could take a look at the visitor's log?" he said pointing to the binder in front of her. Tom knew that if anyone had gone up the elevator with the intention of causing Hank Loughran harm he probably wouldn't have used his real name, but he still wanted to check for any name signed in around the time that Dr. Chu had said Hank had died.

At first she looked at him like he was speaking in tongues and then a worried look crossed her face. "Ooh, I don't know if I can do that." She shot a glance towards here co-worker, who was still on the phone.

Tom put on his most earnest smile. "I just want to see if my grandfather made it in to see his friend on the third floor. I haven't been able to get a hold of him today."

As he finished the other woman, whose name badge said 'Gladys,' hung up the phone and frowned at Tom. She looked from him to Helen with an expression that seemed to say 'What is it now?'

"This gentleman would like to see the visitor's log," Helen said to her.

Gladys' frown grew into a scowl. She looked over Tom's shoulder at the line forming behind him. Visitor's hours were winding down and family and friends were heading for the exits.

Gladys shook her head. "Sorry, the binder can't leave the desk," she said impatiently.

"Just a quick peek? I'll give it right back."

"Sir," she said haughtily, "You're holding up the line." She then shot a look over her shoulder like she was trying to catch someone's eye.

Tom was on the verge of pleading his case further when a tall black man with a shaved head in a security uniform stepped up to his right shoulder. His nametag said 'G. Williams.'

"Can I help you with something sir?" Williams said.

Tom looked at Gladys who shot him a smug look and then over his shoulder and said, "Can I help the next person in line?"

Tom stepped aside and turned to face Williams the security guard. "Are you the supervisor?"

Williams shook his head and used some not-so-subtle body language to draw Tom away from the desk. "No," he said. "That would be Mr. Thompson and he's left for the day."

Tom dug a business card out of his wallet. "Look, a friend of mine died here today."

"I'm sorry to hear that," Williams said.

Tom realized that people probably died here every day. He regrouped and said, "I know that's not unusual given where we are, but I was hoping to find out if he had any visitors before he died."

Williams shot him a glance. Tom noticed they were moving towards the front entrance. "And why would that be?"

Tom struggled to find the wording that would not sound paranoid or crazy. "Just to put my mind at ease...Do you have cameras on the elevators?"

"We do, but I wouldn't be able to check anything without Mr. Thompson's approval."

Tom handed the business card to Williams who gave it a quick glance and then continued towards the exit. "Could you give this to Mr. Thompson and tell him I'll be in touch."

Williams nodded. They were at the entrance and Williams stopped. He looked up at Tom and said, "I can do that, sir. Is there anything else?"

Tom knew he was expected to go quietly and knew there was nothing else he could do right then. "No, that's it. Thank you."

"Have a good night then, sir."

Tom went out the door and as he glanced over his shoulder he saw Williams walking back towards the desk keying something into the radio microphone on his shoulder.

Was he crazy? Tom wondered this as he made his way to the parking garage and entered the stairwell. Something about Hank's demise, however expected, didn't seem right. He came out on the second level and made his way over to his car, which was one of only a few left on the ramp.

He had his key chain in his hand and was about to push the button to unlock it when he thought he heard a footstep behind him. Right before he could turn around, the back of his head absorbed a blow that knocked him forward. The sound of whatever hit him echoed inside his skull and it felt like his head was on fire. He saw only red as he slid down the driver's side door and onto the cold pavement. He rolled over on his back and his eyes went from double to single vision a few times until they settled on a sort of shimmering reality.

There was a man standing over him, holding a forty-five. Tom tried to focus and slowly he recognized who it was. He had grown a beard and was wearing a hat but he knew right then that Mike Manzella was pointing a gun at his head.

Chapter 9

"Hey asshole," Manzella growled as he pointed the gun at Tom's head.

The previous spring Tom and Whitey Brennan, with the help of Whitey's two sons, had stormed a strip club that Manzella had been running drugs through, putting a serious crimp in his business. Manzella had disappeared and his partner, the 'legitimate' face of the business, had been killed. Tom had often wondered what happened to Manzella, if he would ever re-emerge. And now here he was.

Tom's head was spinning. He tried to move but Manzella leaned in closer after looking over his shoulder. "Don't," Manzella said. "I got half a mind to do this right now but you and I got to have a little talk."

Tom was taking a quick inventory of the situation. His vision was clearing up but the back of his head was screaming. He also felt a warm wet spot under his head on the otherwise cool pavement. He was flat on his back with his head towards the front of the car. He still had his keys clutched in his left hand.

"I don't know what the fuck-" Tom started to slur.

"Shhh," Manzella hissed, pushing the barrel of the gun right into Tom's forehead. "Let's cut the bullshit. You know who I am and I know who you are and what you did."

"I—"

The barrel was pressed down farther, pushing Tom's head back into the blood pooling underneath it.

"Look Donovan," Manzella continued, "You fucked me. You cost me a fortune in inventory and got Shields killed. He was a pain in my ass but a useful one. And add to that the people I work for now don't forget shit."

With that Manzella brought up his heavily bandaged left hand, it was clear he was short one pinkie.

"So before you figure you got nothing to lose here and do something stupid I need to show you something." Manzella then reached gingerly into his coat pocket and took out a photograph. He turned it over and held it up to Tom's face.

It was a picture of Tom's mother's house on Taunton Avenue. Tom's fear turned to anger as he looked past the gun into Manzella's hard brown eyes. He fought the urge to try to grab for the gun and waited.

"Good, I got your attention," Manzella smirked. "Here's the deal, You tell me who was with you the night you fucked up my thing at the club or I pay a visit to your mom and tell her how I killed her piece of shit, ex-cop son and then put a bullet in her too."

Tom's mind was racing. He could either give up Whitey and his sons or get his mother killed. Of course a guy like Manzella and the animals he worked for might just kill his mother out of spite anyway. The only option he saw was not to die tonight.

Off in the distance someone's tires squealed in the garage. Manzella flinched but then brought his gaze back to Tom. Once again he applied pressure to the gun. "Well?" He said. "What's it going to be Donovan?"

Tom closed his eyes like he was resigning himself to something. In his left hand he fingered his key chain and tried to remember which button was which. There might not be a second chance.

He pushed one of the buttons and heard the trunk of his car pop. Fuck, he thought to himself. Manzella looked up but didn't move the gun.

Tom's finger moved to the button below it and pushed that one. The car's panic alarm started blaring.

"What the f-" Manzella uttered. That was all he got out though. As he looked up his aim moved away from Tom's face and Tom used that second to bring his right hand up into Manzella's groin and grab hold of Manzella with every ounce of strength he could muster. He brought his left hand up from underneath the car and grabbed the barrel of the gun and deflected it just as it went off.

The blast was deafening. The slug went into the pavement inches away from Tom's head. The impact seemed to shake the very ground where his head was. The heat from the barrel was burning Tom's hand but he didn't dare let go.

With a hand still holding his manhood in a death grip, Manzella let out a grunt and sank down on top of Tom. Tom knew he wouldn't be able to keep up an extended struggle in his current condition so he let go of the gun barrel and grabbed Manzella's shooting hand by the wrist before Manzella could withdraw it from under the car. Tom jammed Manzella's hand up into the rusted metal of the car's undercarriage, once, twice, three times and then raked it across the metal. Manzella lost his grip on the gun and it bounced away further underneath the car.

Tom was starting to fade and Manzella broke the grip he had on his private parts. He could feel his eyes starting to roll back as Manzella painfully stood up. The last thing he remembered was Manzella looking off at something and then turning and staggering off. Tom couldn't fight off the inevitable anymore; he closed his eyes and faded out.

Chapter 10

Tom opened his eyes. Hank Loughran was standing in front of him with a pack of smelling salts cracked open. Looking past Hank, Tom could see Hector Ramiriez and his corner celebrating wildly. The salts snapped him to and he looked up at Hank.

"I'm proud of ya kid. You gave it everything you had," Hank said, removing Tom's headgear.

Tom felt the disappointment wash over him. He had come so close to taking his weight class. Technically, he was better than Ramirez, but Ramirez was faster and stronger. In the third round, Tom had known he was down on points and tried to out-slug Ramirez but that had only played into his opponent's strength and Ramirez finished him off with a flurry that left him dazed at the bell. He remembered something his late father had told him years before:

"You may think that you're the toughest guy in the neighborhood, but eventually you're going to run into somebody tougher or bigger or who fights dirtier than you do. Eventually you are going to get your ass kicked." Such was his father's lecture after Tom had been sent home from school for pounding on a bully who had been giving one of Tom's friend's grief. Tom closed his eyes again.

When he opened them he was in a white, brightly lit room. It took him a second to realize he was in a hospital and Hank was still dead. Then he remembered his run-in with Manzella.

"Jesus Christ. You look like shit," came a voice from his right.

As Tom's eyes slowly adjusted he looked over to see his Uncle Sam standing off to the side. He tried to sit up but his head was pounding.

"Take it easy," Sam said.

"Sam," Tom said hoarsely, "where..."

"You're in the ER at Buffalo General. They found you in the parking ramp next door and brought you right over." Tom noticed that his uncle was still in his uniform but his tie was loosened and the collar button was undone. His demeanor was somewhere between concerned and angry. "So, do you want to tell me what happened?"

"I got mugged."

Sam took a step closer to the bed and shook his head. "Nope. I mean what really happened. You still had your wallet and cell phone on you."

Tom suddenly thought about his mother and the threat that Manzella had made. Immediately he regretted lying to his uncle and realized he might be in over his head.

"I'm sorry," he started. "Do you remember the Shields thing last year?"

"How could I forget? We never did charge anybody with his murder." Sam furrowed his brow. "Jesus, don't tell me you had something to do with it?"

"Not like that, no. It seems that his partner blames me for what happened to his drug and prostitution business."

"Manzella?" Sam said raising his voice. He then stared hard at Tom. "And did you?"

Only a handful of people knew that Tom and the Brennans had wreaked havoc on the strip club that Manzella was doing business out of; Sam was not one of them. Tom had to tread lightly here. He had to tell his uncle about the threat to his family but wasn't sure if he was ready to tell his uncle the whole story.

"I'm not sure why he thinks that," he said, carefully maintaining eye contact. "All I know is he blames me and he thought I was holding out on him."

Tom could tell Sam was getting impatient, that he knew there was something Tom wasn't telling him. The room was quiet for a moment with the only sound coming from outside where a doctor was being paged over the PA system.

"He threatened mom," Tom said breaking the impasse.

"What?"

"He had a picture of the house and said if I didn't tell him what I knew he was going to kill her."

Sam's look of impatience suddenly turned to shock. "What the fuck have you done?" he asked.

Tom already felt guilty, but now his stomach hurt almost as much as his head. He didn't know what to say. Tom's Mother, Rosalie Dipietro Donovan was Sam's only sibling and he had sacrificed a great deal to help Rose and Tom throughout Tom's life.

Sam grabbed his overcoat off of a chair and started to pull it on. Something seemed to cross his mind and his expression softened somewhat. He stepped over to the bed and looked down at Tom. "I'm going to pick your mother up and take her to my house. There will be a uniform here in about fifteen minutes so you just lay here and don't do anything stupid. Tomorrow morning you and I are going to have a talk."

"Uncle Sam, I am so sorry," Tom said.

Sam firmly put a hand on Tom's arm. "You rest up kid. We'll get this taken care of." Then Sam turned and left the room.

Tom settled back into the pillow and felt a tightness on his scalp. He brought his hand up and felt the gauze wrapped around his head. Just then a man walked in wearing a white coat over blue hospital scrubs. He was smooth-faced and looked like he was just out of high school.

"Good, you're awake," he said moving over to the bed and setting a large envelope down. "I'm Dr. Edwards." He took a light out and checked Tom's pupils.

Doctor? Tom thought. I must be getting old. "What's the prognosis Doc?"

"Well, you're going to live," Edwards said without a smile. He put the light in the pocket of his lab coat and picked up the envelope. He walked over to a panel on the wall and flipped a switch that illuminated it. He pulled two x-rays out of the envelope and clipped them on to the panel. "You should really think about not letting people use your head for a piñata though. You have a concussion."

Tom looked at the spot on the x-ray where Edwards was pointing with a pen. There was a mark where Manzella had struck him, probably with the butt of the gun he was carrying. "How bad is it?"

"Well, by itself, not too bad." Edwards moved the pen to the other x-ray and another mark on the image of Tom's skull. "But then, there is this little guy. When did you get that?"

Tom remembered receiving that blow from a woman named Katrina Bedford the previous spring. Bedford had been acting as a de-facto bodyguard for Gary Shields' wife. "About a year ago," he said.

Edwards turned to Tom. "And did you have any tests done after that knock? CAT scan, EKG?"

Tom shook his head no. "I didn't think it was that bad."

Edwards turned back to the panel and snapped off the light. He took the x-rays down and started to put them back in the envelope. "That's what I figured." he said.

Punk, Tom thought. "So you run a couple of tests and I can leave?"

Edwards turned back once again and grew serious. It was a look that belied his youth and gave him an air of authority. "Mr. Donovan, if I let you leave here tonight there is a chance that you may black out on your way home or worse you may get home, fall asleep and not wake up. You are going to be admitted as soon as they're ready for you upstairs."

Tom felt himself flush slightly. He thought about arguing but could tell the kid wasn't going to budge. And just as quick as he had turned it on, Edwards expression returned to the fuzzy cheeked, unassuming ER resident who had first entered the room.

"Okay, Doc."

Edwards told him to sit tight and left the room. As soon as the door closed Tom stood up and caught himself right before he fell. He waited for the room to stop spinning and then found his clothes, cell phone and wallet in a plastic bag on a shelf under the bedside table. His jeans and his coat were still filthy and damp from when he had gone down in the parking ramp. It was all he had though, so he gingerly put them on and then looked at himself in the mirror. He thought he looked like a Revolutionary War re-enactor with the bandage around his head. He carefully removed the wrapping and pulled the gauze pad off the back of his head. It stung slightly as it pulled the dried blood off of his wound. He found another pad on the stand and opened it up and gently dabbed it at the back of his head. There was just a small amount of fresh blood on it when he examined it so he knew it wasn't oozing out.

By all rights he knew he should stay in the hospital. He couldn't though, not with Manzella running around loose threatening his family and friends. He had to get to his car and his gun. He couldn't sit still while the trouble he had made had put his mother and others in harm's way.

The cold air helped him clear his head slightly as he exited the hospital. He had walked the block to the entrance of the parking garage just in time to see his car hooked up to the back of a police tow truck turning out onto Carlton Street and then heading downtown in the general direction of the BPD impound lot. Of course, he thought. His car would be considered part of a crime scene. He checked his phone; it was 1:38 AM. He could probably get a cab in about a half an hour. He was just about to dial information when a blue Nissan came out of the ramp, hesitated and then made a beeline for him.

His ex-girlfriend, Erica Gilford was behind the wheel, looking angry. She locked up the brakes practically on top of Tom's feet and leapt out of the car and glared at Tom over the roof of the car.

"What do you think you are doing?" she asked sharply.

"Erica, I have to get to my apartment." He was looking back at her unapologetically.

"You have a grade two concussion you idiot. You're supposed to be held for observation."

"You don't understand..."

"Don't understand what? You have to save the world tonight or die from a cerebral hemorrhage?"

"I didn't think you were working tonight." Erica was, in fact, a nurse at Buffalo General. Tom had asked if she was there and was relieved to find out she was off for just this very reason.

"Kathy called. She said they brought you in and you were in rough shape. I was on my way here when she called again and said that you disappeared. I found your car just as the police were taking it away. Did you know they have your parking space taped off? Tom, What the hell is going on?"

Tom walked over to her passenger side door and put his hand on the latch. He began pleading with his eyes. "Look, I'm not going back. I can't. Just give me a ride home and I'll explain or I walk away right now."

Erica frowned and it looked like she was on the verge of crying. That would have been unusual; she very seldom cried as far as Tom could recall.

She started to say something and bit it back. Then she shook her head and said, "Get in."

Chapter 11

Erica was mostly silent on the ride to Tom's apartment. Rather than suffer the silence, Tom gave her an abridged version of his run-in with Manzella and the threat to his mother. Halfway through his story Tom started to wonder if he had put Erica in danger also. He thought he saw a flicker of fear in her face as she made the same realization.

Erica and Tom had met when Tom had visited Buffalo General when he was still a cop. He had come in to take a statement from a liquor store clerk who had been assaulted during a holdup. They struck up a conversation and hit it off. The next time Tom was at the ER on another matter he worked up the courage to ask her out.

Erica was thirty-two years old and had been married to a physician's assistant for a year when she was in her late twenties. She chalked it up to a 'youthful mistake,' when she realized her husband was not only extremely controlling, but a germaphobe on the verge of being neurotic. The PA had relocated to North Carolina and she had moved on.

Tom and Erica got along great and she moved into his apartment on St. James after they dated for about nine months. She worried about him and his job but he was faithful and considerate and physically they clicked.

The trouble started when Tom lost his badge. She tried to be supportive but found Tom growing increasingly withdrawn and sullen. They managed to live together for another eighteen months but at the end they were little more than roommates. She told Tom that she loved him and would always care about him but she couldn't live with his ghost. Tom didn't put up a fight and let her go; a decision he would often regret.

He had tried to bridge the gap after the Shields' case ended. The events that had unfolded reminded him that life was a tenuous thing and he had to put his own self-pity aside and reach out to the people he cared about. They spoke on a regular basis and had even slept together once after a "Booze Cruise" on the Miss Buffalo.

They both agreed that that reckless night shouldn't be repeated as it would only complicate matters. She knew he was trying to change but there was still some part of him that seemed to be missing. She had dropped the hint that she may have been dating again but never seemed to want to go into much detail.

Instead of pulling up in front of Tom's apartment Erica drove a few houses past and pulled into an open spot. She turned off the car and just looked out straight ahead.

Tom, who had finished his story a few minutes before, didn't know what else to say.

Finally, Erica spoke, "Do you really think that Manzella is going to come after you while your uncle is turning the city upside down looking for him?"

Tom thought for a moment. "I don't know. I just want to be ready. There's no way I could just lay around a hospital while he's out here."

"You just don't get it, do you?" she said sharply, her hazel eyes burning at him.

"Get what?"

"You're not a cop Tom. Let them pick this guy up."

Tom found himself feeling indignant and fought the urge to say something he would probably regret immediately. His head was throbbing and he had lost the will to argue.

"Let me take you back," she said, lowering her voice.

"Erica... I can't. I have too much going on right now." He was also considering the situation regarding his father, Hank Loughran, and the Sons of Eire. "I'll be fine."

She seemed to be at her wit's end. Finally it happened, a tear rolled down her cheek. "God damn it. You won't be happy 'til you're dead will you?"

Tom reached out and put his hand on the hand she had tightly gripped the steering wheel. Had he made a mistake? What could he possibly accomplish in his current condition. It's too late, he thought. He was out and as long as he was out he was going to do everything he could to deal with his current situation.

"Is the first aid kit I left still upstairs?" she asked.

Tom turned to face her; she had regained her composure as quickly as she had lost it. "Yeah, I don't think I've used more than a couple of band-aids."

She opened her door and started to get out. "Come on, let me have a look at that thick head of yours."

Upstairs in the apartment she checked and re-cleaned his wound. She applied a fresh dressing on it and secured it with a length of gauze. She was all business as she finished and led him to the bedroom.

"Get out of those dirty clothes," she ordered. "I'll be right back with some Ibuprofen."

As soon as she left the room Tom went to his closet and took out the case with the 9 mm, took it out and put the magazine in as quietly as possible. He stuck it under his pillow and peeled off his clothes.

He was sitting on the bed when she same back with the medicine and a bottle of water. Tom looked at her and thought again about the time that they had lived together. He then flashed forward and worried about what might happen to her because of his recklessness.

"Erica, I don't want to start an argument, but I think you should stay here tonight."

She looked at him evenly as if she was considering the situation and then said; "I wasn't going to leave you here alone anyway. We can watch out for each other."

She was a special person and Tom once again wondered how he had managed to screw things up. He took the Ibuprofen and laid down. Immediately he felt the evening's events weigh down on him and he felt himself slipping under. One last check under the pillow and he felt the reassuring presence of the Glock. Erica laid down next to him and put her hand on his chest and he was gone.

Tom was vaguely aware of Erica checking his pupils with an LED light she kept in her purse several times through the night. Other than that he slept a heavy dreamless sleep. When he awoke the sun was outlining the shade that Erica had drawn all the way down. He looked at the clock on his nightstand; it was 10:10 AM.

Erica wasn't in the room but he could hear faint sounds coming from the kitchen. He rose, somewhat shakily and found his robe on a chair in the corner. He put it on and wandered down the hall to the kitchen.

He stood in the doorway for a moment and looked at her, standing over the stove heating up some oatmeal in a pan. The smell of fresh coffee caught his attention and he said, "Good morning."

She seemed slightly startled when she turned to face him. "Are you sure you should be up?" she asked.

"Had to get out of bed," he answered. "My whole body was getting stiff."

"Well sit down," she said, gesturing towards the old two seat kitchen table. "I would have made eggs but your refrigerator is pretty bare."

He lowered himself into a chair. "Part of the minimalist bachelor lifestyle."

"That would explain the chunky milk I found too, huh?" She said slicing a banana into the bowl. She brought it over and set it in front of him.

Tom's stomach lurched when the smell of the oatmeal reached his nose. He fought it off and took a spoonful and ate it. Erica came back to the table with two mugs of coffee and a jar of non-dairy creamer. She sat down across from him and looked at him impassively. Tom wondered if there was another lecture coming.

Her hair was slightly damp and her face was makeup free; she had obviously taken a shower. Despite the fact that she probably hadn't slept much Tom was reminded that he had always thought she looked beautiful in the morning.

Tom took another bite of the oatmeal and his stomach was still churning. He was trying to hide it but she saw through it. Her face darkened slightly.

"My offer still stands," she said.

"What's that?" Tom mumbled with a half mouthful.

"Let me take you back to the hospital. I'll tell them you were delirious and you're really not an irresponsible jackass."

Tom sighed. The last thing he wanted to do was upset her again. Still, he thought, there was too much to do.

"I can't."

She closed her eyes and shook her head. "You mean you won't," she said. Now she looked like she was trying to restrain herself. The room fell silent. Tom gave up the charade of eating and put the spoon down.

"Actually, I was hoping you could give me a ride to the office," he said looking down at his coffee.

She had obviously heard enough. She frowned at him once again and stood up. She was almost shaking she was so angry.

"Fuck you," she finally blurted out.

"Erica—"

"You go ahead and pretend that everything is okay and you're in control. Fine, I just won't be a part of it!"

"I don't—"

"I just hope I'm not on duty when they bring your body in for the last time."

She wasn't crying; she was truly angry. With one last scowl at him she left the kitchen. Tom got up and went after her but by the time he got to the living room she had just left the apartment, slamming the door on her way out.

He stood looking at the door as if it was going to open any minute and she would come back in. He soon realized that she wouldn't be coming back anytime soon and decided he had to get moving. He called for a cab and took a shower. His head still ached where Manzella had hit him but the wound had scabbed over. He shaved and got dressed and went to the front window to see if the cab was there. He checked his phone while he waited; he had missed several calls. Two from his Uncle Sam. One from the agency and two from numbers he didn't recognize.

Ten minutes later the cab pulled up out front and Tom started to pull his coat on. He was just about to turn away from the window when a black man in a green army jacket walked up to the passenger's side of the cab and rapped on the window.

What the hell, Tom thought. The cabby rolled down the window and the man leaned inside, showing the driver something. After a moment he straightened up and then the cab sped off. Tom saw the conspicuous bulge of a gun under the army jacket and he started to sweat.

He hurried back to his bedroom and retrieved the Glock from beneath the pillow and stuck it in his belt. Instead of the front door he went through the kitchen and went down the side staircase.

Chapter 12

The air was still, but there was a noticeable chill as Tom peeked out of the side door down the driveway towards the street. No one there. He slipped out of the door and crept to the front of the house and looked around the corner. The man in the army jacket was getting into the passenger side of a black sedan halfway down the block. The car was on the opposite side of the street and had an unobstructed view of the front door of Tom's house.

Tom headed back up the driveway to the tiny back yard and past the ancient garage. He put his hands on top of the chain link fence that separated the yard from the house behind his and took assessment of his physical well-being. His head hurt but he wasn't dizzy; he knew he was running on adrenaline, but he wondered how far it would carry him. He put his left foot halfway up the fence and vaulted over. He came down on the other side and when he landed he saw stars, but a moment later he recovered, none the worse for wear.

Tom walked by the side of the house towards Lafayette Ave. Halfway down the driveway a large dog started barking from inside the house. He quickened his pace and hoped that no one was inside watching him skulking around. He turned left onto Lafayette and walked quickly down to where he was sure he would be past the car watching his apartment on the parallel street. He picked the first house that he thought looked deserted and went over that fence back into the yard of a home on St. James.

He crept down to the front of the house and looked around the corner towards the black sedan. He was about seventy-five yards away and from the angle he was at he could make out a driver with salt and pepper hair and the man in the army jacket looking down the street towards his apartment. He waited until a UPS truck drove down the street in that direction and using it as cover, crossed the street. He turned towards the sedan and took out his phone and pretended to look at the screen as he casually strode towards the car. He closed to about fifteen yards when he looked up and saw the man in the passenger seat glance into the side mirror at him. Tom was running now as a flicker of recognition flashed in the man's widening eyes. Tom had his gun out and closed the distance before the man could reach into his coat.

"Don't!" Tom growled. "Both of you, keep your hands where I can see them.

The black man in the passenger seat looked up at Tom with malice in his eyes. The driver, who Tom could only see from the shoulders down, complied by putting his hands on the wheel.

"Who the fuck are you two?" Tom continued.

"I hope you got a permit for that thing Tommy," said a familiar voice from the driver's seat. Tom tilted his head so he could see into the car. It was Detective Ernie Santiago.
He raised his eyebrows and said, "Permit or no, would you kindly not point it at Detective Foster?"

Tom at once felt foolish for being so paranoid. He lowered the weapon and dropped his head. When he looked up Foster was still staring daggers at him.

"Hop in Tommy," Santiago said. "We should have a talk."

Ernesto Santiago had been a patrol sergeant when Tom came on the job. A few years later he was plain clothes and then he made detective just before Tom lost his job. Tom had worked with him in E district for a couple of years and knew he was a good cop.

Tom heard the locks click open and he climbed in the back seat and sat behind Foster. Santiago turned around and looked at him. "Man, you look like shit," he said.

"Rough night," Tom replied.

"I heard. So I guess you know why we're here then?"

Tom didn't reply. He had a feeling his uncle had something to do with it.

Foster made a noise with his lips and Santiago shot him a look. Santiago spoke again, "Well, this is a prime example of what he's worried about Tom. Somebody cracks your head open last night and you are out here running around the street waving a gun."

Tom felt his face grow hot. "Ernie, I'm sorry you got sucked into this, but I can take care of myself and I have some shit I've gotta take care of."

Santiago turned forward and looked at Tom in the rearview mirror. He thought for a moment and then said, "Not to bust your balls, but do you have a permit?"

"Yep, concealed carry and everything. It's in my wallet if you want to see it."

Foster let out a grunt and shook his head.

"What is his fucking problem?" Tom said flatly.

Before Santiago could reply Foster turned around in his seat to face Tom. "How in the fuck did you get a pistol permit?" He asked heatedly.

"It's my constitutional right, asshole."

"Like you are some kind of constitutional scholar," Foster scoffed.

Tom turned towards Santiago and said, "I'll ask you again Ernie, what is this guy's fucking problem?"

"Jimmy-" he started, looking hard at his partner.

"Just wondering if you had a flashback is all?" Foster said cutting him off. "Seein' a black face and you with a gun in your hand."

So that was it. No surprise there. There was still a segment of the population that would always look at Tom Donovan skeptically. "Fuck you. You weren't there."

"True that," Foster said turning back towards the windshield. "But I was with the Housing Authority for two years and I know how shit goes down in the projects."

Tom thought about arguing his point further but decided it was probably pointless.

Santiago was flushed and glaring at his partner. The air in the car was heavy and silent.

After a moment of silence to allow everyone's pulse rate to return to normal Santiago turned around and looked at Tom again. "I don't suppose you were planning on spending a quiet afternoon at home then were you?"

"I could lie to you Ernie and say yes. But you know I would just leave again. Although now that you know to watch your mirrors I won't be able to get the drop on young Foster here."

"What... fuck you!" Foster said without turning around.

"Knock it off!" Santiago said to both of them.

Again the car went silent. Tom knew he shouldn't have made the dig but he was tired of being judged by people who didn't know him. Finally he cleared his throat and said, "Say since you guys are done here and you chased off my cab, how about giving me a ride to the Agency?"

Santiago looked at him incredulously and then smirked. Foster shook his head and said, "Man, you've got balls." Santiago started the car and Foster shook his head again.

No one spoke in the ten minutes it took to travel down Delaware Avenue to the Agency. As he pulled up in front of the building, Santiago broke the silence. "You know I have to tell him don't you?" Tom knew he was referring to his Uncle Sam.

"I'll call him," Tom said without hesitation. "I talked to him last night and he knows I don't want to sit still."

Santiago was looking at Tom in the mirror and after a moment said. "Nah, don't worry about it Tommy. I think it would be better coming from me, if it's all the same to you."

Tom nodded and said, "Alright Ernie. I'm sure I'll be speaking to him soon enough anyway." He got out of the car.

On his way to the building's front entrance he threw a look over his shoulder and it appeared that Santiago was giving Foster a lecture. That was a consolation to Tom; at least the cops he had known while he was on the job knew the truth and had his back.

As soon as he entered the reception area of Frederickson and Associates, Grace Frederickson looked up and her eyes widened. Simon Willis, another retired cop who worked for the agency was standing next to her desk and followed Grace's stare towards Tom.

Willis let out a low whistle and said. "Damn son, what's it take for you to call in sick?"

Well, the whole office knew, as usual.

"'Tis but a scratch," Tom replied.

Grace opened her mouth to speak but before she could start her husband Cal was filling up the doorway to his office. Sensing his presence she glanced over her shoulder at him. He did not look happy.

"A moment please, Mr. Donovan?" Cal said, crooking his finger.

As soon as Tom crossed the threshold Cal said, "Close the door," and took a seat behind his old wooden desk. They stared at each other for a few moments; Tom didn't know where or with what to start so he was more than happy to let Cal take the lead.

Cal finally exhaled and said, "So, what happened last night?"

Tom broke eye contact and looked at his shoes. "I got mugged," he said.

Cal sighed audibly. "Seriously? We're going to do this?"

Tom looked back up. "Do what?"

Cal shook his head and continued; "Let me help you out. Vernon Thompson, who as you may know is the Director of Security at Roswell Park, and I go back to our days in the fourth precinct in the eighties. His man told him that you were at Roswell last night in an agitated state."

Tom said nothing and waited.

"Nothing yet?" Cal continued. "Okay. The only reason you are sitting here right now instead of lying in the morgue is that they were watching you in the garage to make sure you left under your own volition. One of his officers actually was the one whose arrival scared your assailant off."

Tom could feel his face getting hot. How much did Cal know? He was just about to speak when Cal went on.

"As a matter of fact, there is surveillance video of the parking garage. Not close enough to your car to see what actually happened but there are cameras in the stairwells and I got a good look at your assailant."

How much did Cal know? Just about everything about last night as it turned out. Tom had never told Cal the entire story about his involvement in interrupting Manzella's business but he knew his boss had suspicions.

"So why didn't he just pop you?" Cal asked, bringing Tom back to the present.

It was Tom's turn to exhale now. "He wanted to find out what I knew about the club?"

"Like what?"

"Like who broke in, tied up the manager and found the drugs."

Cal frowned deeply, creating a crease in his forehead. Tom fully expected the 'I knew it' speech coming up but somehow he restrained himself. Cal let his brow relax and leaned back in his chair. "Knowing how Goddamned stubborn you are, I am going to guess that you were not forthcoming with any information and somehow managed to get the gun from him, since they found it under your car." He looked to Tom for confirmation.

Tom nodded and said nothing.

Cal's gaze intensified. He went on, "So what does Manzella have on you that would make you bolt out of a hospital bed with a concussion and be out on the street strapped with what looks like a 9mm under your jacket the very next day?"

"He threatened my mother."

"Did you tell the police? Or mainly her brother, Captain Dipietro?"

"Yes-"

Cal kept going, "So what good could it possibly do, you running around half-cocked?"

Tom opened his mouth to speak but nothing came out.

Cal continued, "Oh, and Vernon Thompson says he would stake his reputation on the fact that nothing untoward happened to your friend on the fifth floor."

Tom was stunned. Cal knew much more than he had hoped he would. He knew he didn't have enough to justify reinvestigating his father's death and had hoped to keep it to himself, for now.

Cal sat back in his chair and studied Tom through lowered eyelids. "One thing I learned as a homicide detective is not to let things get too personal Tom."

"Meaning what?"

"If you get too personally involved it clouds your judgment and you start to see things that aren't there."

Tom was at a loss. His head was pounding again and his stomach was rising. Before he could respond there was a rather timid knock on Cal's door.

Cal looked up impatiently. "Yes," he snapped.

Grace eased the door open and peeked in. She shot Cal a dirty look and then turned to Tom. "Your uncle is here," she said.

Tom slowly stood up and walked to the doorway. He briefly felt like he was back in high school, doing the perp walk from the principal's office to his uncle's car. There standing in front of Grace's desk in street clothes was his Uncle Sam, looking none too pleased.

Tom made eye contact with his uncle. He saw a mixture of pain and aggravation in his face. Then Sam looked over Tom's shoulder.

"Calvert," he said coolly.

"Captain," came the response, without sounding any more friendly.

Sam looked back at his nephew and said, "C'mon, let's go."

Chapter 13

Tom and his uncle rode down Delaware Avenue in a strained silence. A few times, Sam had seemed like he was on the verge of saying something but each time he bit it off. Tom thought back to the year after his father died and Sam had moved Tom and his mother to a house he owned on Taunton Place in North Buffalo.

Tom had a hard time adjusting to his new high school. He was withdrawn and sullen and had started to turn somewhat rebellious towards authority figures. He had found himself in the principal's office on more that one occasion. One winter day, he had gotten into a fight in his gym class and was facing a three- day suspension. For some reason, maybe because she was so upset, his mother had asked her brother Sam to pick up her wayward son. Sam was a lieutenant in the Buffalo PD at the time and showed up at Tom's school in uniform and in a police cruiser. Tom's schoolmates were sure Tom was going off to jail and more than a few of them thought it was about time.

They hadn't spoken until Sam pulled out of the lot. Finally he glanced over at his nephew and said, "Look, I get it, you're pissed off. I would be too. But nothing is going to be gained by getting kicked out of school."

Tom's jaw tightened as he looked out the window at nothing in particular.

"You realize if you get kicked out of this place you will just have to start over somewhere else?"

"That would be fine with me," Tom muttered.

"Oh yeah? Do you think your mom can afford to send you to private school?"

"Any place but here. Bunch of Dagos thinking that they're all tough guys."

Sam smirked without any mirth. "You realize you're half Italian right?"

Not that Tom missed his old school that much. Frankly he had pretty much lost interest in any kind of institutionalized learning at that point.

They lapsed back into silence at that. Sam didn't speak until they had pulled up to the curb of the house on Taunton. Tom tried the door handle and he found it locked.

He turned to face his uncle, who was looking at him sympathetically.

"You're still grieving," Sam said. "I get it. But none of this is going to change the shitty hand you've been dealt. And I don't think if your dad was around he would appreciate you being such a pain in the ass."

Tom shook his head and found his eyes welling up. "You didn't know him," he said. "As a matter of fact, your side of the family treated him like shit!"

Sam closed his eyes and said, "I'm not going to lie to you Tom. Your dad and I saw things differently. I do know one thing though. Your mother loved him and you and your sister more than anything else in the world."

Sam let that sink in. Tom found himself fighting back a tear. "Will you let me out of the car now?" he said through gritted teeth.

"Sure kid," Sam said popping the lock. "All I'm asking is you think about what you're doing. It's not going to change the past but it sure as hell is going to affect your future."

"Got it," Tom said without much conviction. He opened the door but found Sam's hand on his forearm.

"Oh and one last thing," Sam began. Tom looked up at his uncle whose eyes suddenly took on a dark gaze. "Your mom's been through a lot too.

If this teen angst bullshit gets out of hand I will be back to kick your ass." He let go of Tom's arm.

Tom sat for another moment and then got out of the car.

Back in the present, once they had passed the turn for Tom's apartment, he assumed that they would be going to his uncle's house to prove to his mother he was still alive. He was surprised when they made a right on to Hertel and then a left onto Saranac. They pulled up in front of a modest, one family house with a brick front and a small but well maintained yard. Sam turned off the motor.

"Is this whose house I think it is?" Tom asked.

"Yep," Sam said. "The undertaker himself."

They had arrived at the home of Salvatore "The Undertaker" Manzella, one time under-boss of the Buffalo arm of the mob and paternal uncle to Mike Manzella. Sal and Mike's father Michael "Mickey" Manzella Sr. had been convicted of extortion and bribery charges in an FBI sting in the early eighties and did time in federal prison under the RICO act. Mike Sr. had died of lung cancer while inside. When Sal got out, he returned to the home he had shared with his late wife. His two daughters had married and moved out of town. He was mostly retired, from organized crime by his stint in prison, and from the funeral home he ran his operation out of before the government seized it.

"He's the only connection I can think of to Little Mike," Sam continued. "Besides, I wanted you to see what we've been dealing with all of these years."

Tom didn't fully understand what Sam had meant by the last part of that statement but he knew it would become clear sooner rather than later. His uncle's lessons were seldom hard to understand.

Sam walked up to the front door and rang the bell. A moment later a young, dark-haired man in his mid-twenties answered the door. He was thick-chested and probably a few pounds overweight. He was wearing a black Adidas tracksuit and was sporting a gold chain around his neck. He looked out at them disapprovingly and then propped open the storm door.

"Can I help youse?"

Sam glanced over his shoulder at this nephew and said, "Jesus, look at this guy. Right out of central casting." He turned back to the man in the doorway. "I need to talk to Sal."

The guy looked like he was still trying to decide if he had been insulted or not but then came around. "He's not in," he said.

"Seriously?" Sam said. "So you're telling me that that's your Lincoln Town Car in the driveway? You look more like the Miata type."

Track Suit didn't seem to have an answer for that so Sam pressed on. "Look, I'm an old friend of Sal's. He still sees his friends right?"

Before Track Suit could think of a reply, Sam pushed his way in through the doorway. Tom, somewhat surprised by his uncle's out of character abruptness, snapped to and followed suit. Tracksuit regained his wits and started to reach for Sam's shoulder but Tom stood in his way and squared up with the kid. They were about the same height, with the kid outweighing Tom, but something in Tom's expression told the kid to stand down.

Sam had walked through the living room and stood in the doorway to what looked like a dining room. Tom walked up next to him and saw a heavyset old man with gray skin and dark bags under his eyes. He had brown spots on his bald head and was hooked up to a small oxygen tank that rested on the chair next to his.

"Hiya Sal," Sam said his voice dripping with mock warmth. "You're looking good."

"What the fuck are you doing in my house?" The old man replied with a voice like gravel. He then shot an annoyed glance at the kid in the tracksuit who was now standing to Sam's left.

Sam jerked his thumb at the kid and said, "Your body guard invited us in for cannoli."

The kid started to protest, but Sal waved him off. "Whatever," he said. "Don't you have anything better to do than to harass an old man?"

"Old man?" Sam said raising his hands. "Well, at least you didn't say 'honest citizen' or 'business man'."

Some color came over the old man's face. He grimaced and shifted in his seat. "Just speak your mind then and get out of my house."

"In case you haven't heard, we're looking for your nephew, Little Mike." Sam said.

Sal shook his head. "First of all, I haven't seen him in over a year. Secondly, even if I had I got nothing to do with anything you might want him for."

Sam pointed at a stack of papers in front of the old man. "Yeah, that's right, you're retired. So

I suppose those aren't betting slips or union contracts in front of you?"

Sal sneered now and said, "This shit? It's all my Medicaid stuff. I think they bury you in paper work and hope you die before they have to pay."

Sam jerked a thumb to the young guy in the tracksuit. "And him? He's not your latest goomba in training?"

Sal looked at the kid pitiably. "My sister's grandson. Helps me out around the house."

Tom glanced at the kid who now looked somewhat deflated.

"Alright Sal," Sam said, "I'll take your word that you've mended your ways. Do you have any idea what your nephew has been up to?"

"Only what I hear," Sal said looking down. "The people he works for are animals. They got no sense of honor."

Sam scoffed at that. "Honor? Like the Cosa Nostra of old?"

Sal turned toward Sam and returned the scoff. "Like you guys are that much better. Some of your co-workers downtown were our best customers."

If the dig bothered Sam he didn't show it. He turned to Tom and said, "You want to hear about honor? Sal and Big Mike got sent up when their cousin Pete ratted them out to the feds. And do you know why? Pete got his feelings hurt when he found out Big Mike was banging his old lady."

Salvatore Manzella was seething now. "I don't know where he is and I don't care. Even if I did know I wouldn't tell you, you fucking overpaid, sanctimonious Boy Scout." He looked at his grand-nephew and said, "Get these assholes out of my house."

The kid puffed himself up a little and tried to look tough but Sam had already turned around and was headed to the door with Tom at his heel. They let themselves out and walked out to the car.

Once they were in, Sam stopped himself before he turned the key in the ignition and turned his head to look at Tom. "You see what you're dealing with here? The God damned mob thinks Mike Manzella is crazy."

Tom didn't know what to say. He'd known that Manzella was linked to some dangerous people but hadn't seriously considered the fallout that might come from screwing with him. In his heart, he knew that even if he had, he probably would have done the same thing.

Sam turned the key, put the car in gear and pulled away from the curb. "And here we are.

Ironic that you work for Cal Frederickson now. It's come full circle."

Tom didn't follow. "What are you talking about?"

"Did Frederickson ever tell you about his run-in with Mike Manzella?"

"He said they had a history."

Sam shook his head and said, "A history? That was his last case as a cop. We had Manzella for a homicide in Black Rock and your boss decided to cut corners. Long story short, a witness recanted, said Frederickson coerced him. The DA kicked the case and Manzella walked. Frederickson was going to get kicked out of homicide but he retired instead. That's the history."

Tom was feeling defensive. "But Manzella got picked up on a drug rap—"

Sam interrupted, "Yeah and he did five years of a ten year sentence instead of life which is what he should be doing. And now here's Little Mike running loose on the streets again."

Tom didn't offer any more resistance. His uncle was truly agitated and Tom knew whatever he said wouldn't help. He knew that there was probably more to the story, Cal's side in particular, but he was tired and his head ached again. He let a few minutes go by and then asked, "Where are we going?"

Sam had regained his composure. "We're going to my house. You are going to show your mom that you are still in one piece and apologize for scaring the crap out of her. After that I'm going to take you home and you are going to stay there until I tell you it's safe to stick your thick head outside."

Chapter 14

Tom spent the afternoon and evening with his mother and uncle. When his mother seemed placated his uncle offered to drive him home. They rode in silence all the way to Tom's apartment until his uncle pulled up to the curb.

"Tom," Sam began, "I know this is hard but I really need you to stay put for a couple of days until we find Manzella."

Tom felt completely drained, all of the fight had left his body. "I will. And Sam, thanks for taking care of mom."

His uncle smiled wanly. "Family, right?"

"Right," Tom replied.

He walked to the front door of his house and went into the vestibule. From the window next to the door he watched his uncle edge up to another car part of the way down the street and stop. The angle was severe but he saw the other car's window roll down and the driver had a brief exchange with Sam who then drove off. Tom locked the door and went upstairs. At first he was irritated and a little embarrassed that his uncle would have someone sitting on his house but then he thought of his downstairs neighbor, Caroline and her son Brandon. Enough innocent people had already been hurt and the extra security for the people around him was a good thing.

After a hot shower and a couple more Ibuprofen he turned in. He slipped under almost as soon as he hit the pillow. He slept deeply but still had some fitful dreams, the details of which were hard to recall but he remembered they all seemed to have a dark tone.

He woke up the next morning and rolled over to check the clock on his nightstand; it was 9:38 AM. He had slept for a solid twelve hours. His head still ached but not as sharply as the day before and his stomach seemed to have settled down to the point where he actually felt hungry. He found his phone in his jeans pocket and when he pulled it out he realized the battery was dead. As soon as he put it on the charger he saw that he had missed four calls; One from Sherry, one from Frederickson and Associates and two from a blocked number. None of the callers had left a voicemail.

He called the Agency first and got no answer. That was unusual, Grace was a stickler for answering incoming calls. Then he called

Sherry's cell and again, no answer. He put a pot of coffee on and had a bowl of dry cereal and pondered what he was going to do while he waited for his uncle to release him from his unofficial house arrest.

He poured himself a cup of coffee and went into the dining room and fired up his laptop. After he skimmed over some of the news sites he sat back and thought about how to better use his time.

He found an old article about the Manzella family and the end of their criminal enterprise in the eighties. He got out his notebook and started listing the names of family members and associates. It was a short list, with most of the people on it were either deceased, incarcerated or past their prime.

Tom pondered that for a while. If Mike Manzella hadn't contacted his uncle Sal, what were the odds that he had turned his back on the entire family? Of course, uncle Sal could have been lying through his teeth.

He had to move forward, to do something else. Again he returned to the Son's of Eire website looking for a thread. He clicked on all of the tabs on their home page and then on a tab marked photos. The top of the page noted that there were

247 photos posted. Oh well, Tom thought, what else do I have to do?

Even though most of the photos were fairly recent, it appeared that the bulk of the membership of the Son's of Eire was on the down side of fifty. That would make them old enough to have been around in the late eighties. A club as old as the S.O.E. probably had volumes of photos stored somewhere but the ones that Tom was looking at were from the digital age. It would have been nice if someone had been thoughtful enough to scan some of the older pictures and post them.

There were pictures of various parties, charitable events and Irish dancers. Tom was just about to exit the photo gallery when he saw a familiar face; the guitar player from the night he had visited the club. It was a picture of the man onstage with a guitar and microphone serenading the faithful in the club's bar. The caption read "Seamus McNally" and was dated a few years ago. From the angle it didn't appear that McNally knew he was having his picture taken.

Tom remembered how McNally had frozen when they had made eye contact at the club. He had then retreated and moments later the gorilla had come out to give Tom the bum's rush. His thoughts were interrupted by a knock on his living room door.

He froze momentarily. Would Manzella be reckless enough to try something in broad daylight with half of the Buffalo PD looking for him? He went through the living room and peeked through the curtain.

It was his downstairs neighbor, Caroline. She looked up through the window and gave a little wave. Tom opened the door and she stepped in.

Caroline was in her late twenties, stood about 5'4" and was a little on the heavy side. She had a round, attractive face with blue eyes and streaked blond hair. She was usually in a good mood, albeit tired-looking. She was a single parent of an eight-year-old son, Brandon, who had Asperger's syndrome. Brandon's IQ was off the charts but the Asperger's made it hard for him to communicate and he could be what Tom's teachers would have termed 'disruptive' in a normal classroom setting. Caroline worked a full-time job and devoted the rest of her time to her son. Tom had a great deal of respect for her and had gotten used to Brandon's tics and idiosyncrasies. He had never seen Brandon's father or had asked Caroline about him for that matter.

"Did Mr. Spanikos talk to you?" Caroline asked.

Teddy Spanikos was their landlord. The gruff son of Greek immigrants, he was in his fifties and at times could be a little off-putting. He wasn't seen too often and that was fine with Tom. The small repairs around the apartment he could handle himself, and as long as the rent was paid Spanikos left him alone.

"No, but I have been kind of wrapped up in something the last couple of days," Tom said. "Why? What's up?"

"He was here with a guy from the gas company yesterday. They were looking for a leak. I think they came upstairs."

"Did they find anything?"

"No," Caroline shook her head. "But it still freaked me out. Did you smell anything?"

"Not really."

They both stopped when they heard the door at the bottom of the stairs open. Tom tensed up and his heart almost stopped when Caroline leaned back into the hallway at the sound of boots ascending the stairs. She must have caught the person's eye because the footsteps stopped halfway up.

"Hi." Caroline said cheerfully.

"Hello." Sherry Palkowski's voice sounded a little tentative. She finished climbing the stairs and entered the room.

Tom made the introductions and Caroline caught his eye and raised her eyebrows and smiled. Not even close, Tom thought. Tom could tell Sherry was upset about something so he explained to Caroline that Sherry was a co-worker. Caroline took the hint and excused herself.

"What's wrong?" Tom asked as soon as he closed the door behind Caroline.

"The FBI's Cyber-crimes Unit was at the Agency this morning looking for Brian."

"Jesus Christ!"

"They missed him by a half hour, but they ransacked his office and took most of his equipment."

Tom thought for a moment. Brian had been poking around in places that he probably shouldn't have on his behalf. A wave of guilt washed over him.

Sherry seemed to be reading his thoughts. "Apparently he has been getting involved with some serious stuff Tom. It goes beyond anything he may have been doing for us."

She had used the term 'us.' Sherry knew what Brian was capable of and had probably used his services on occasion herself.

Tom came around. "What did Cal say?" he asked.

"What could he say? If he threw a fit he could be charged with obstruction or as an accessory."

Tom thought about that and then said, "No wonder I couldn't get a hold of Grace this morning. Are the Feds still there?"

"No. They went through Brian's office and had a talk with Cal, then they left."

"What about the rest of us?"

"What do you mean?" Sherry asked.

"Are they taking statements or anything?"

"Not yet, but they made a list of all the Agency's employees. All the same, I thought I'd come here in person. I may be paranoid but who knows who they are listening to."

Tom let out a long breath and looked at his friend. "This is not good. I have a feeling there's going to be some kind of fallout for the rest of us." He had a thought then; "Jesus, and with you going into the academy next month."

Sherry gave him a crooked smile. "Well, it is what it is. I have a feeling though that Brian knew what was coming and was covering his tracks."

"What do you mean?"

"He was in this morning. It was weird. He was in a bit of a rush but he was smiling, like he knew something nobody else did. He also seemed like he was focused, like he was on a mission. How often do you see that?"

"True," Tom said, affording himself a smile.

Sherry dug into her coat pocket and pulled out a small electronic device. "Oh, and before he left he said to give this to you."

"What is it?"

Sherry handed it over. "It's an mp3 player."

Tom looked it over and said, "Like an I-pod?"

Sherry rolled her eyes and smiled. "Yeah, but don't call it an I-pod. I did and Brian went into an explanation about it not being an Apple product and then some rant about corporate fascism. I think he cut it short when he remembered he was on the run."

Tom found the power button and turned it on. It took him a second to figure out the menu but he did and started to scroll through the songs.

"Holy crap," he said. "It's like he memorized my CD collection."

"Yeah, he said there's no accounting for taste. He was especially disparaging of the Pogues and the Dropkick Murphys."

Tom allowed himself another smile and considered the gift.

"There was one thing..." Sherry started.

"What's that?"

"After I promised him I would deliver it to you personally, he got all cryptic. He said to make sure you check out the 'classics.'"

Tom looked up at Sherry as he tried to decipher what that meant. "What are you going to do now?" he asked.

"I think Cal's trying to keep it 'business as usual.' I have to do some legwork for Bob Stanley." Then she thought of something. "That can wait though if there is anything I can help you with."

Tom said, "No I'll be alright."

"I knew you'd say that and I won't push it, but you scared the crap out of us the last couple of days."

Tom felt his face flush.

"Just remember Tom," Sherry continued, "You've still got friends."

"Thanks Sher, I know." They had a quick somewhat awkward embrace and she was gone.

Tom went back to the kitchen and got another cup of coffee. He looked at the mp3 player and thought about what Sherry had said about Brian and his odd message. He realized he didn't own a pair of headphones to listen to it but after inspecting the device he found a USB plug that he could attach to his laptop. He went back to the dining room and plugged it in.

After a few moments the device synced up with his media player and the full menu of songs came up. He picked a Social Distortion song that he hadn't heard in a while and clicked play. He scrolled through the rest of the songs until something caught his eye. The song *Space Oddity* was written in all capital letters. He thought for a moment and then said, "Major Tom," out loud. Brain was the kind of person who seldom addressed his co-workers by their given names and Major Tom was one of his favorite nicknames for Tom.

He clicked on Space Oddity and the song started. It was the original by David Bowie, recorded in 1969. He was just about to turn it off when the music stopped and Brian's voice came on.

"Tommy boy, as you probably have heard by now I have had to resign my position at Frederickson and Associates. Not to worry though, the reason for my abrupt departure has little to do with what the government has their panties in a wad about."

Little to do, Tom thought. That meant it had a lot to do with it.

Brian continued; "I got you a going away present though. Even though this mp3 player is filled up with all of that beer-soaked Celtic punk rock that you seem to favor, there are a couple of read-only files in its memory. Just go back to the menu to open them up. Some interesting stuff about your friends at the Son's of Eire and a little more information about Detective Kennedy. Enjoy, my friend, and don't worry about ol' Brian. I am leaving this town for better things." There was a pause and Tom thought Brian had finished but then he stated again. "I hope this helps Tom. You're a good dude and I liked working with you. Peace." Then the song came back on.

Tom did as Brian had instructed and sure enough there were files stored under the data section of the player. He opened one marked Sons of Eire and scrolled through it. There were ten pages of information that would take awhile to go through.   Then he clicked on the file marked 'Kennedy.' He picked up his phone and called his uncle.

After letting Sam reassure him that his mother was fine he got to the point. "Uncle Sam, I'm going stir crazy here. I was thinking about blowing town for a couple of days."

Sam hesitated and then said, "I'm not sure if that's a good idea kid."

"Look, I'll be out of the way and only you and I will know where I'm going."

"And where would that be?"

"I have an old friend in Florida. I was thinking about looking him up until this blows over."

Chapter 15

Donovan had one credit card to his name. Between the flight, booked at the last minute, and the rental car, it was going to be nearly maxed out. Since his car was still in the police impound lot he took a cab to the airport in Cheektowaga, arriving at 5:40 AM, an hour before his flight was to board.

Despite being the middle of the week and the crack of dawn the flight was full. Mostly families heading off for spring break, attempting to escape a winter that seemed to have lingered longer than usual. Tom thought the seats were more cramped than he remembered and the cabin had all of the ambiance of a Greyhound bus, but it would serve its purpose.

As soon as they reached altitude and the seatbelt light went off Tom booted up his laptop. He opened up the file Brian Dinkle had sent him regarding retired Detective Bernard Kennedy.

Kennedy had put twenty years in, the last five as a detective. He had a fairly unremarkable record, no major busts, no citations. Shortly before he retired in 1995 he had gone on a thirty-day medical leave for undisclosed reasons. There was nothing in his jacket about being injured on duty or any other health problems. Tom didn't like to make assumptions but he had seen similar situations when he was a cop. A fellow officer would have a personal problem, family, emotional, alcohol or other that would result in a department ordered leave. The more sensitive the problem, the more vague the information in the file. In the ten years that he had been a cop Tom had seen the handling of personal issues improve vastly. The department was getting away from the days of its "Just suck it up" mentality. A lot of the veterans had bristled and thought things were getting too soft, but the reality was that the job could be incredibly stressful and if unchecked, small issues could become big ones.

There was also a picture of Kennedy in uniform with no date on it. Judging by the haircut and the color on the picture Tom guessed it had been taken decades ago. There was no telling how Kennedy may have aged in the interim.

After a forty-five minute layover in Charlotte it was back on board for the second leg to Fort Meyers. Tom used the time to transfer information from the file to his notebook. As he did this he also thought of a strategy on how to approach Kennedy. He didn't know the man from Adam and due to the lack of information in the report on his father's death, he had no idea how much time or effort Kennedy had put into the investigation. He had never even heard of the man before Brian started digging.

Kennedy had retired at the age of forty-eight. That would make him seventy-six. His wife had passed away four years ago and he went from being a "snow bird" to a full time resident of the state of Florida. Brian had provided his current address as well as the make and model of a car registered in his name.

11:05 AM, the plane started its descent into Fort Myers. As the air pressure changed in the cabin Tom tried to swallow and get his ears to pop. Suddenly he felt dizzy and his stomach turned over. He had felt a little odd when they landed in Charlotte but this was much worse. The concussion was still bothering him. The elderly man seated next to him seemed to pick up on this.

"Are you alright, son?"

It took Tom a few seconds to realize the man was speaking to him. When he glanced over he regained his composure and said, "Been a while, but I get a little motion sick sometimes."

"You lost your color there for a second. I thought I was going to have to grab a bag for you."

Tom felt the heat as soon as he exited the plane and walked down the jet way. The air conditioning was on in the terminal but the humidity was still there. He hadn't checked any bags so he went straight to the rental counter.

As soon as he left the terminal he could feel his tee shirt stick to his back. The thermometer said it was 89 degrees but after leaving Buffalo and a rainy 42 degrees it may as well have been 120. The compact car he rented was hot as an oven and he dropped the windows and cranked the air conditioning as soon as he got in. He pulled out the directions he had printed the night before and followed the signs to I-75 North.

Punta Gorda was a small city, located across the bay from Port Charlotte. It had a modest, clean downtown with shops and small businesses but was mostly residential. Tom's directions took him West, towards the Gulf of Mexico, where tracts of one-story houses gave way to groups of manufactured homes. All of them seemed to have some kind of private waterway or lake. He found Burnt Store Road, which seemed to be being built up to handle more residential and retail properties and moments later he came up to Harborview Homes.

Tom had a separate map for the Harborview community. All of the mail was delivered to a common area by the park entrance so he had dug a little on a real estate web-site to find out how the lots were numbered. Bernard Kennedy lived towards the back of the property on one of the narrow, winding roadways.

He passed the community center, with its screened in pool and shuffleboard courts and noticed that despite the mid-day heat, many of the residents were out and about, walking small dogs and riding three wheeled bikes. The snow birds were probably used to the weather. No one in the park looked to be younger than seventy-five so Tom tried to look as inconspicuous as possible and act like he knew where he was going.

After one wrong turn Tom found Sunset Lane and pulled up in front of Kennedy's address. The driveway and carport were empty; it looked like the widower was out. Tom had the sensation he was being watched and sure enough when he climbed out of the rental car he found himself almost face-to-face with Kennedy's next door neighbor who stood looking at him with an electric hedge trimmer in his hand. He was a heavy-set man in Bermuda shorts and a New York Mets tee shirt with the permanent sunburn many of the residents seemed to have. It must be a dermatologist's dream down here.

The man eyed him for a moment and then said, "Hello."

"Hi," Tom said cheerfully. "I was looking for Bernie Kennedy."

"Oh, are you a relative?"

Tom had his story ready; "Um no, he and I have some mutual friends back in Buffalo."

"Is that right?" The man wiped his brow. "Are you a cop too?"

"I am." Tom didn't know how, maybe the way he carried himself, but even after three years of being an ex-cop, people still identified him as one. "Bernie is kind of a local legend back home."

The old man thought for a second and then said, "He doesn't talk about it too much."

"That's Bernie, he always let his work do the talking." Tom realized he may be laying it on too thick and decided to rein himself in.

"Well, if it's Wednesday, he's probably at the club. Some of the guys are in a golf league and they tee off at 3:00."

Tom checked his watch, it was 3:17. "Sorry, which club was that?"

The man made a face and Tom wondered if he was getting suspicious. He imagined the locals were probably on guard for con men and criminals, the kind of dirtbags who prey on the elderly.

"I just wanted to say hello and then I have to get back to Ft. Meyers for a fishing trip."

The man considered this and said, "It's called Seminole Lakes. It's only a couple of minutes from here."

Twenty minutes later Tom was cruising through the parking lot of the club. As he expected, there were more than a few Lincoln Town Cars, seemingly the car of choice for retired Floridians. After a few more minutes he found Kennedy's car by the plate number that Brian Dinkle had supplied him. He had forgotten to ask Kennedy's neighbor if the golf league played nine or eighteen holes. Given the heat and the average age of the participants Tom guessed it would probably be nine. Tom had tried golf when he was younger but had found it to be too slow for his liking. He kept boxing when he became a cop and participated in some exhibitions, mostly against the fire department. He did remember that nine holes could take between two to four hours.

He thought about going into the club and waiting at the bar. Then he looked down at his clothes, short-sleeved button down shirt and jeans, and realized he would stand out. He would have to find an unobtrusive vantage point and wait for Kennedy to come out. He worried that it might be a while if Kennedy and his buddies stayed for drinks and dinner.

There was a little plaza across the main drag from the country club. Tom found a donut shop, got a cup of coffee and found a parking space where he could watch the club entrance for Kennedy's car.

Kennedy must have forgone dinner with his cronies because at 6:25 PM Tom saw his Town Car making a left onto Route 41, the opposite direction from Kennedy's home. Tom eased out into traffic and followed Kennedy from a couple of cars behind.

41 split into two one way streets as it entered downtown Punta Gorda. Kennedy made a left onto West Charlotte Avenue and after a few blocks pulled into the lot of a Roman Catholic Church. Had Kennedy found religion?

Tom pulled into the lot and parked where he could watch. Kennedy got out of his car and walked over to a side entrance. There were other people there standing around, more than a few of them smoking and Tom knew where he was.

When he was a cop he had known a handful of fellow officers who were in Alcoholics Anonymous and a few more who should have been. He knew enough about it to understand that the group valued its anonymity and traditions. He was about to do something he knew he wouldn't be proud of.

At 7:00 PM the smokers all stubbed out their butts and went down a stairwell and into the church basement. Tom slid out of his car and jogged over to the stairs, went down and then inside.

There were about thirty people in the room seated in folding chairs lined up facing a lectern. Tom was scanning the room for Kennedy when a voice came from beside him.

"Hi, first time?" The voice belonged to a man of about fifty, balding in a well worn work shirt.

"In Florida?" Tom asked.

The man chuckled slightly. "No, an AA meeting."

Tom realized he had to invent a cover story on the fly. "No. I've been to a few up north."

The man must have read Tom's uncertainty for something else because he said,

"Relax, grab a cup of coffee. This is a great group. Nobody's here to judge you."

Tom smiled and said nothing.

"I'm Jesse," the man said extending a calloused hand.

"Terry," Tom said.

Just then the leader gaveled the group to order. Jesse pointed over to a table with a coffee urn on it and Tom went over and grabbed a Styrofoam cup and filled it up. There was a seat open in the back row next to a tired looking girl who was fidgeting with her hair. She didn't look up when Tom sat down.

The twelve steps were read and the basket passed for coffee and expense money. Tom mostly mimicked the people around him so as not to stand out. A man got up and told his story for about thirty minutes. He started by telling the group how messed up his life was. Tom thought it was amazing that someone would tell a room full of strangers all of the awful things he had done and wondered what the point was. Then the man talked about hitting bottom and realizing he was an alcoholic, and how he got sober. The man said he had been clean for ten years, Tom was surprised that all of the man's drinking stories were so fresh in his memory after all that time.

Then he realized he could still recall all of the shitty things he had been through in his own life with clarity and it made sense.

When the speaker was finished the leader asked if anyone had anything to add and a few hands shot up. Tom had stopped listening though as he had spotted Kennedy a few rows up and to his left. Kennedy seemed to be in a kind of trance with his arms folded and his eyes half closed. He wondered if Kennedy's personal leave from the police force was related to a problem with alcohol.

Before Tom knew it, the sound of chairs moving brought him out of his trance. Everyone around him was standing up and then the group recited the Lord's Prayer. Tom had to mouth the words as he hadn't said it since had attended a Catholic grade school in the eighties and couldn't recall much of it after the first few lines.

Then people started moving towards the exit. He had one eye on Kennedy from about twenty feet away when he almost bumped into Jesse.

"Wasn't that bad was it?" Jesse asked smiling.

"Not at all."

"A couple of us are going to the diner around the corner for coffee, wanna come along?"

Tom hesitated. He already felt like a heel for intruding on these people and now he didn't want to be rude on top of it. He also saw that Kennedy had made it out the door and didn't want to let him get too far. "I would but...ah...my uncle and I are going fishing before the crack of dawn tomorrow and I need to get some sleep."

Jesse smiled again and held out his hand. "No problem," he said. "Next time then?"

Tom shook his hand and said, "Sounds good." Then he hustled out the door.

Kennedy was just finishing up a conversation with another man, also in his seventies. Tom sidled up to him as he made his way to the Town Car.

"Excuse me?" Tom said.

Kennedy turned and half smiled. Something like a shadow came over his expression. It was like he was expecting someone from the group that he recognized, not some stranger. "Yes," was all he said.

"You wouldn't happen to be from Buffalo, would you?"

Kennedy just looked at him, expressionless now.

Tom continued, "Sorry, my name is Terry Donahue. I'm a cop from Buffalo."

"Is that right?" Kennedy said.

Tom hadn't known what to expect but Kennedy was making this hard. "Sorry to jump out at you like this but I grew up in South Buffalo and I started out in South division after the Academy. I saw your picture at the station and read a little bit about you and the guys you worked with back in the day."

"That was a long time ago," Kennedy said smiling slightly. "What brings you to Florida?"

Tom had already considered his back-story. "My uncle has a place in Port Charlotte. I've been down since the weekend doing a little fishing."

"And you're in the program?"

"Six months now."

"Been in a few years myself." Kennedy looked towards his car. "You know the pressure of being a cop and a member of the CIA."

"CIA?" Tom asked.

Kennedy looked at him incredulously. "You're from South Buffalo and have a name like Donahue and you've never heard the term CIA?"

Tom had no idea what Kennedy was saying. "Um... no."

Now Kennedy actually laughed and said, "CIA stands for Catholic Irish Alcoholic."

Tom let out a nervous laugh. "Say Mr. Kennedy-"

"Bernie," Kennedy interjected.

"I hate to intrude but would you like to get a cup of coffee?"

Kennedy thought for a moment and Tom wondered if he had rushed things. Then Kennedy spoke, "Tell you what. I have to go home and let the dog out. Why don't you follow me and I can show you some stuff I have from my time as a cop."

"That sounds great," Tom said, barely catching himself from sounding too enthusiastic.

Fifteen minutes later they were at Kennedy's home. The sun had almost set into the Gulf some five miles away. Kennedy pulled into his carport and Tom parked in front. Tom walked up the drive while Kennedy unlocked the side door. He held the door open and called in, "Come here, you little shit."

A small, ancient dog gingerly stepped into the doorway. Kennedy snapped a leash onto his collar and picked up the dog and set it on the ground at the foot of the steps.

"I hope you held it until I got home, you little bastard."

Kennedy looked up and saw the confused look on Tom's face and said, "Oh, he and I have a love-hate relationship. He was my late wife's dog and we never got along. She made me promise to take care of him and now we are seeing who is going to outlive whom." He held the leash out to Tom. "Would you mind? I have to hit the can and he doesn't even need the leash, but the guy next door is a prick and I don't need any grief from the resident's association."

"No problem," Tom said as he took the leash.

The dog walked to the edge of the driveway and sat down. Kennedy had gone inside and Tom could hear him moving around the mobile home. Tom wasn't sure if the dog had to go or even if he knew he was outside for that matter. He tried tugging on the leash a little but the dog just sat there. Finally after what seemed like about ten minutes the dog stood up, walked over to a rose bush and relieved itself.

He picked up the dog and climbed up the two steps to the side door and knocked.

"C'mon in," Kennedy said.

Tom opened the door and set the dog down and took off the leash. He held up the leash and looked for a hook or something to hang it up.

"Where do you keep—" Tom stopped. Bernard Kennedy was ten feet away from him, pointing a snub-nosed .38 caliber at his chest.

"Who the fuck are you?" Kennedy said evenly. Tom looked into his eyes and thought he saw a little fear.

"I told you, my name is Terry-"

"Bullshit!" Kennedy interrupted. "Your whole story sounds like crap. If you've been here since the weekend out on the water, how could you still be white as a sheet?"

Tom had raised his hands slightly to show Kennedy he meant no harm. He wondered if he should try to continue the lie.

"Well, who are you and what the fuck do you want?" Kennedy raised the gun and now pointed it at Tom's head.

"Wait," Tom said.

Kennedy's hand was shaking. He seemed to be trying to control it with little success. "Start talking or I'll put one in your fucking skull," he said.

Tom raised his hands higher. "Jesus, I'm not armed."

"Doesn't matter," Kennedy went on. "In Florida we have this 'Stand Your Ground Law.' Since you entered my home and threatened me I have every right to defend myself with deadly force."

Fuck, Tom thought to himself. "My name is Tom Donovan. I was a cop but now I'm a PI."

A little of the color drained from Kennedy's face as he started to connect things. "Your Hugh Donovan's grandson," he said.

"Yeah, and Tom Donovan's son."

The gun dropped slightly and the rest of the color left Kennedy's face. It looked like he had seen a ghost.

"Look Kennedy, all I want is a little information."

Kennedy seemed to snap out of his reverie. "I should shoot you on principle," he said waving the gun. "Your family was nothing but a giant pain in the ass when I was on the job."

Goddamned Hugh, Tom thought. "I have no doubt about that," he said.

"And I would have never believed you were a cop except I read about you killing that spade in the projects a couple of years ago."

Tom could feel his blood rise but still said nothing.

Kennedy continued, "I guess the apple doesn't fall too far from the tree."

Now Tom couldn't hold back. "What the fuck is that supposed to mean?"

Kennedy smirked. "C'mon, how old were you when your old man died?"

"Fifteen."

"How much did you know about his work?" Kennedy said the last word with a trace of sarcasm.

Tom was used to feeling defensive about his own past but this was new territory. "I knew he was with the Laborer's Union."

"Goddamned no-show job is what that was. Do you know what he really did?"

Tom just stared back at Kennedy. He hated where this was going. "That's not what-"

Kennedy raised the gun again and Tom stopped. "He was a leg breaker and a messenger for good old grand-pa, that's what he was."

Tom was furious now. Things had gotten off track. He always had suspicions about his father, especially as he got older. No one had ever said it out loud to him though.

"What do you think about that?" Kennedy asked.

"I'm thinking I should take that gun and shove it up your ass."

Kennedy hadn't been expecting that and took a step back. After a moment he recovered his bravado and said, "Well, that's not going to happen, so why don't you just get the fuck out of my house and go fuck yourself."

"Just answer one question," Tom said.

Kennedy exhaled and said, "What?"

"You know the accident report, the one you never signed off on? They found an empty pint bottle of whiskey in the car and you just assumed he was drunk. What happened to the toxicology report and the autopsy?"

Kennedy's jaw went slack. "I worked that case ... You don't know what you're talking about," he said with diminishing conviction.

"Bullshit!" Tom raised his voice. "Nobody knows where my father was that night or who he was with and it looks like nobody tried to find out either. It looks like you spent all of twenty minutes looking into it. Tell me it wasn't because of some bullshit grudge you had with my family."

Kennedy lowered the gun again and seemed to be replaying something unpleasant in his mind.

"I was a cop for ten years and I never saw such a bullshit piece of police work. How the fuck did you get away with that!" He took a step towards the old man.

Kennedy brought the gun up again and said, "Stop!"

Tom saw Kennedy fading and went for the opening. "Tell me about it Bernie. What happened?"

"I got a call on my day off from the precinct. They said they had a body in the canal and they were short-handed. My captain said I had to take it."

Tom waited for him to go on.

"Turns out the Chief of Detectives wanted me on it specifically and at first I couldn't figure out why, especially when I found out who it was."

"What did that have to do with it?" Tom asked.

Kennedy smirked. "Your dad, granddad, Whitey Brennan and I had a long history together. Most of it wasn't good."

Tom was curious but didn't want to let Kennedy get off track. "Tell me about the investigation."

"It was by the book. The only thing was I had to run everything through downtown and the Chief of D's."

"Why?"

"Well I didn't know at first but then I found out that the information was being shared with the Fed's."

"Why would they want to know about it?"

"They never told me but when I brought up the fact that your dad was last seen at the Son's of Eire Social Club they sat up and took notice."

An alarm went off in Tom's head. "Were they protecting someone at the Club?"

Kennedy looked down and his face fell. "You just came to the same conclusion I did."

Tom stepped closer and raised his voice. "So what did you do?"

Kennedy looked back up at him, his eyes were misty. "I started asking questions and they told me to drop it. I blanched a little and then the Chief told me in no uncertain terms that I could drop it and move on or some things in my jacket were going to come back and bite me in the ass."

"What things?"

"I wasn't always the picture of sobriety you see now. Back then I was having a lot of problems. One more strike and I would have been out on my ass with no pension."

Tom looked at Kennedy differently now. He was sober but he carried the weight of his past sins. He had thought he was going to confront a conspirator, but instead found himself with a patsy. He thought he should feel angry but instead felt pity for the old man more than anything.

"Kid," Kennedy said.

Tom looked back at him now. Kennedy looked beaten but at the same time he seemed relieved, possibly the cathartic effect of confession.

"Yeah."

"It's no secret me and your family didn't get along. But I am sorry it went down like that."

"I know. Me too." Tom went to the door and realizing he still had the leash in his hand, dropped it on a chair.

Chapter 16

Tom stood up and tried to work the kink out of his neck before he reached up into the overhead compartment for his bag. After leaving Bernard Kennedy alone with his past, he drove directly to the airport in Fort Meyers. He had eight hours to kill before his flight. He found a deserted gate and tried to sleep on one of the hard plastic seats. He woke up with still tired, with his entire body stiff and sore.

As he left the gate he fished his phone out and turned it on. There were two messages on his voicemail. The first was from Grace Frederickson, asking him to call as soon as possible. He checked his watch; it was after seven PM, no one would be at the office and he really just wanted to get home and get some sleep. The second message was from his uncle Sam who said his car had been released from the police impound lot and his keys were with his downstairs neighbor. Sam also requested a return call but said it wasn't urgent.

Tom got a taxi at the cabstand and was back at his apartment just before eight. He took a quick look up and down the street but didn't see anyone sitting in a car. He wondered if the cops were still sitting on his house, waiting for Manzella to surface. He climbed the stairs, entered the foyer and knocked on the downstairs apartment door.

Brandon answered the door, wearing Captain America pajamas and holding a TV remote control. He looked up at Tom blankly. His features were like his mother's, blond and fair, but he was thin and tall for his age.

"Hey bud, is your mom home?" Tom asked.

"Brandon," Caroline said as she entered from the dining room. "What did I tell you about opening the door?" She was wearing a t-shirt and sweat pants and when she got close enough Tom thought he detected the scent of a cleaning product.

Brandon didn't reply. He just turned and went back to his program.

"Sorry Caroline," Tom said. "I just got back in town and my uncle said he left my keys with you."

She smiled at him and said, "Don't worry about it. I wasn't expecting you so soon. Your uncle said you would be gone for a week or so."

"Change of plans," Tom smiled back.

She reached into a ceramic bowl on a small table near the door and took his keys out. "Here you go."

"Thanks Caroline. Again, sorry for the hassle." He turned towards the door.

"Oh," she said. "I know what I wanted to tell you. The guy from the gas company came back this morning and said he had to get back in the basement. He said it was just a follow up."

"Was the landlord with him?"

"No, he was by himself. I heard him knocking around on the back stairs and I told him I had to get to work and he said he hadn't found anything anyway and then he left."

Tom went upstairs and took a long, hot shower and then went to his room and sat on the edge of the bed. It was then he noticed the closet door was open about an inch. The latch on the door was old and the door had to be held closed in order for it to catch, a habit Tom had gotten himself into and now did without thinking. He walked over to the closet and pulled the door open. Something didn't feel right. He couldn't be sure but it seemed like something had been moved since he packed for his trip. He reached up and took the accordion file with his personal papers off the shelf and reached to the spot at the back of the shelf.

It was gone. The box that held the black .38 Smith and Wesson revolver that he had found among his late father's things when he was cleaning out the basement was gone. He stood for a moment and then stepped over to the bed and threw himself on the floor. He looked under the bed and found only dust and an old magazine. His new Glock was gone too, case and all.

"Shit," Tom cursed himself for not getting a gun safe or finding a better hiding place. He pulled on a pair of jeans and t-shirt and went to the kitchen. The door to the back stairs had been forced open. He went downstairs and knocked on the door.

Caroline opened the door with a quizzical look that changed to fright when she saw Tom's strained expression. Tom could tell that he was scaring her and tried to get a hold of himself.

"What's wrong?" She said.

"The guy from the gas company." Tom tried to control his breathing. "Did he have ID?"

She thought for a moment and said, "Yeah, he had a laminated badge with his picture."

"Did you notice a name on the badge?"

Caroline shook her head and looked like she was going to tear up.

Tom knew from his years as a cop that the average person doesn't notice details like that. The distractions of everyday life tend to block that part of a person's consciousness.

"Okay, don't worry about that," he said trying to sound soothing. "Do you remember what he looked like?"

She was trying to compose herself. Brandon had come into the kitchen and was looking concerned. He had probably picked up on the tone of the conversation.

"Tall... white or gray hair. Glasses... I don't know... late fifties?"

This was pointless right now Tom thought. He wasn't going to file a police report anytime soon, especially to report the theft of an unlicensed handgun. The Glock he would have to report eventually. He remembered then that he was still standing in Caroline's doorway.

"I'm sorry," he said. "It's just that a couple of things look like they were taken from my apartment."

She put her hand up over her mouth.

"Don't worry," he said. "Nothing really important was taken. I'll call my uncle in the morning and we'll get this figured out."

"Tom, I'm so sorry,"

"No, no, no, don't be. The guy had ID. What were you supposed to do, follow him around?"

He spent a few more minutes assuring her that she was blameless and then went back upstairs. He thought about the description she gave. It ruled out Manzella, who Tom doubted would take the trouble to break into his apartment instead of just putting a bullet in his skull. Was it an associate of Manzella's? It didn't fit. Or did it have something to do with his poking around the Son's of Eire and their membership? In any event it didn't feel like a random burglary; some one didn't want him carrying a gun.

Chapter 17

Tom barely slept that night. He kept cursing himself for not securing the guns. The .38 was bad enough but the Glock was brand new and registered in his name. The phony gas company man had thrown up another impediment in a week that he now felt was spiraling out of control.

He finally gave up on sleep at dawn, got out of bed and made a pot of coffee. His head still hurt and he still felt fatigued so his heart wasn't into going for a run. He logged onto his computer and killed time mindlessly surfing the net.

At eight AM his phone buzzed, the office. Tom reluctantly answered it.

"Yeah."

"Donovan?" Tom was surprised it was Cal and not Grace. He hesitated.

"Are you there?" Cal said gruffly.

"Yeah, sorry boss. Got in late last night."

"You need to get in here."

"Now?"

"Your presence has been requested by Special Agent Miller of the Federal Bureau of Investigation." Cal said dryly.

"Can it wait Cal? I've had something come up."

"Nope."

Tom thought for a second and said, "Is he sitting with you in your office right now?"

"Yep."

"I'll be there in thirty minutes."

>>><<<

Tom walked into the reception area of Frederickson and Associates and saw Grace Frederickson sitting at her desk with her arms folded in front of her looking peeved. It was then he noticed that her computer was missing from her desk.

When she saw him the expression on her face turned to one of concern. "Tom, are you alright?"

"Nice to see you too, Grace."

She frowned slightly and said, "Sorry, it's just that you look like shit and me being the compassionate person that I am I decided to ask about your welfare."

Tom felt stupid for being short with her. "Sorry," he began, "It's been a rough couple of days."

She jerked her thumb in the direction of her husband's office and said, "I think they're about to get rougher."

Seemingly on cue, Cal came out of his office trailed by a man in his early thirties wearing an inexpensive gray suit and a maroon tie. The man was built solidly and had a crooked nose. He looked more like a bouncer than a Fed.

"Tom Donovan," Cal began, "This is Special Agent Miller of the FBI's Cyber Crime Unit." Tom noticed that Cal looked equal parts exhausted and aggravated.

Miller stepped up to Tom but neither one extended a hand. "Mr. Donovan, would you step this way please?" He gestured down the hall towards the conference room.

Tom turned to follow Miller but shot a quick look towards Cal. Cal narrowed his eyes in a look that Tom couldn't decipher.

The conference room was actually a small office at the end of the hallway to the right of the reception area. It had a small table and a laptop connected to a projection screen on the wall. When they entered the room there was another agent seated at the table, this one tall, thin and impossibly young looking.

"Kyle, could you give us the room for a minute?" Miller asked.

Agent Kyle looked up from his laptop, which he had wired into Grace's computer tower. It took him a moment to realize what had been said but then he stood up and said, "Sure, I'm going out for lunch. You want anything?"

"No, I brown bagged it."

As the other agent was leaving Miller took off his jacket, revealing thick arms, broad shoulders and a 9 mm clipped to his belt.

"Have a seat Mr. Donovan," he said pointing to a chair.

Tom sat down and Miller opened up a file folder and picked up a pen. He looked up and made eye contact with Tom.

"What?" Miller said.

Tom realized Miller was probably wondering why he was smiling, given the gravity of the situation. "You just don't look like what I imagined a cyber-crimes guy would look like." He gestured to his own nose but was referring to Miller's, "You do any boxing?"

Miller shook his head but didn't return the smile. "No, I got this when I was playing hockey at MIT. I got cross checked hard enough to break my cage."

Miller was all business and Tom knew he was trying to stare him down. He had done the same thing himself dozens of times when he was on the job. He knew the time for small talk was over.

"You know why we're here?" Miller said.

An open-ended question deserves a vague answer. "Something about our computers?" Tom replied.

A corner of Miller's mouth curled up. "Brian Dinkle in particular," he said.

Tom sat expressionless and waited.

Miller looked back down at the file in front of him. "How much do you know about what Mr. Dinkle does here?"

"Research mostly."

"Mr. Donovan, I am aware that you used to be Buffalo PD. And I am not going to insult your intelligence and hopefully you will return the favor."

"Meaning what?"

"Meaning that you would probably be aware if Mr. Dinkle had been doing anything of an unlawful nature while doing this research," Miller said with a sarcastic tone on the word "research."

Tom knew he had to choose his words carefully. He had no idea how much the Feds knew and wouldn't until Miller played his hand. If he outright lied and got caught he could lose his PI license or, worse, be charged with obstructing justice. "Brian did his thing and frankly it was a little over my head. He never told me where he came up with the stuff he did."

Miller waited but Tom stopped there. He still looked hard at him across the table. Finally he said, "Did you ever ask Mr. Dinkle to obtain information from a source that you knew would be restricted?"

Tom felt his neck getting warm. "Like?"

"Let's cut the crap Donovan. Your friend Brian Dinkle got a little sloppy on one of his forays into government archives and left a trail that we followed here."

Tom already knew the answer but asked anyway. "What does that have to do with me?"

Miller shook his head. "You really want to do it this way? One of the things Dinkle was nosing around in was a case from '89. Does that ring any bells?"

Tom's apprehension was replaced by a renewed curiosity with what the FBI's involvement was in burying the investigation of his father's death.

"Actually that does ring a bell. Why would the FBI bury a report on a suspicious death that same year?"

Miller was caught off guard for a moment but then he said, "I don't know what you're talking about... or how that's relevant."

Tom thought he saw Miller look down ever so briefly but before he could say anything Miller went on, "Besides I am the one asking the questions here. Was Dinkle acting on your behalf?"

"Yeah, he was. But I didn't tell him to incur the fucking wrath of the FBI while he was at it. I had no idea."

The room fell quiet and they just stared at each other for a moment.

Miller had composed himself. "So I can assume that you do not wish to cooperate freely with this investigation?"

"I thought I just did," Tom said sitting back in his chair.

Miller started writing on a legal pad. He paused and reached into his shirt pocket and took out a business card.

"Fine," he said. "You know how this is going to go. We are going to find Mr. Dinkle, arrest him and prosecute him under the Computer Fraud and Abuse Act. If during the investigation any accomplices are identified, they will also be prosecuted." He held the card out. "If your memory or common sense improves, give me a call."

Tom raised his eyebrows, took the card and put it in his pocket. There were all kinds of questions he wanted to ask Miller but he knew they wouldn't be answered. One thing was certain though; his father's death and the following investigation were looking more suspect all the time.

Chapter 18

"How bad is it?" Tom asked.

Cal had followed him down the left hallway to Tom's office. He'd closed the door softly behind him as he entered. Tom sat down, but Cal remained standing. At least now some of the tension had left his demeanor.

"That depends." Cal said.

"On?"

"Oh, a number of things. I've been warned against it by Agent Miller but I have to ask you, how deep are you into what Brian was doing?"

It was time for full disclosure, Tom decided. He'd already caused enough trouble and he owed Cal at least letting him know what he was involved in. "Brian was doing some digging for me. I didn't tell Miller, but I know he got into the DOJ and FBI database. How far? I don't know."

Tom thought Cal would explode but he just seemed to be considering something.

Finally he asked, "Digging into what?"

Tom exhaled and said, "I recently found out that there might have been more to my father's death than the official story."

"Go on," Cal said.

"Long story short, the official report was altered and a lot of it was buried. The FBI was involved."

Cal frowned. "Say what?"

"Bernie Kennedy signed off on the case and turned everything over to the Chief of Detectives at the time. The ME's report went missing and the rest of the file is pretty thin. I got confirmation from Kennedy himself that the Feds had taken an interest."

"Kennedy? He's still alive? He retired about twenty years ago. When the hell did you talk to him?" Cal caught himself raising his voice and reined it in.

"Two days ago. This all started when an old family friend told me the story about the night my Dad died. The trail led to Kennedy and the Irish social club on the south side. That's what Brian was doing for me."

Cal closed his eyes and rubbed his temples. "I know it's always bothered you not knowing for sure about your father..." His voice trailed off.

"But?" Tom prompted.

Cal shook his head. "Nothing...I just wish you could have gone about it a little differently."

A wave of guilt washed over Tom. Once again his pursuit of the truth had created unintended consequences. He looked up and Cal was looking at him now with what seemed like pity, which made him feel worse.

"Cal I am sorry. This has bothered me since the night it happened. I know my dad was no angel but he was still my dad. I think the Feds were protecting somebody at the Sons of Eire and I want to know why."

"Alright, alright, don't get all maudlin on me," Cal said. "I'm going to tell you something now that can't leave this office." He lowered his voice to a near whisper. "Apparently the stuff Brian was doing for you, and for the agency for that matter was just the tip of the iceberg. You know that seminar he went to last week?"

"The one in Tampa?"

Cal smirked. "Yeah, well that was all bullshit. There was no convention. It seems our Mr. Dinkle has fallen in with some bad company."

"Who?"

"A group of hackers. Call themselves The Digital Underground. Brian came back, said hello and then cleaned out his office. He's been a step ahead of the Feds and they're pretty pissed off about it."

Just then someone knocked on the door and Cal almost jumped. The door opened and Cal's nephew, Travis, stuck his head in. He nodded at Tom and then looked at Cal. "Yo, boss, the Federales say I'm clear. Just wanted to tell you I'm going to go out on that thing we talked about."

"Fine," Cal said. Then he thought of something and held up a finger to his nephew. "Call me at home later."

"You got it." And Travis was gone. Cal turned his attention back to Tom. "I have a feeling this will blow over in a couple of days," he said. "Brian's in the wind and he took everything with him. What did Miller say to you?"

"Nothing really. I told them I didn't know how far up their asses Brian had crawled. I think they're done with me for now."

Cal allowed himself a smile. "Okay. Get out of here then. I already told Sherry and the others to keep up business as usual for now. You," he pointed at Tom. "I want you to go home for a couple of days and I will call you when the suits are gone."

"No problem," Tom said.

On his way to his car Tom called his Uncle Sam who told him that Manzella's whereabouts were still unknown. The police had officially (and in some cases, unofficially) contacted all his known associates who weren't either dead or in jail and came up empty. Tom now had more time to kill: he wasn't needed at the agency and apparently Manzella had felt the heat and left town or was laying low. He really regretted losing his gun more than ever because he would have bet money that Manzella would eventually resurface. He headed home to plan his next move.

Every instinct told him that all roads led back to the Sons of Eire, Loughran, Kennedy, and the information Brian had given him. Plus the rude reception he got the night he went there. Maybe it was time for another look. He checked the time; it was a little after four PM. His head felt better and he was feeling restless so he decided to head to the gym. He got his bag from the front closet and headed out.

He arrived at the gym on Elmwood and checked in. When he was in the locker room getting changed he realized he had left his cross trainers in the trunk of his car so he went out to retrieve them. He walked through the entrance and almost crashed into Sal Manzella's grandnephew.

They stood for a moment and looked at each other. The kid looked nervous, Tom thought to himself.

"Hey," Tom started, "It's..."

"Mark, Mark Salerno," the kid said.

Another pause. Then Tom jerked a thumb over his shoulder in the direction of the gym and asked, "You a member here?"

Tom thought he saw a flicker in Salerno's eyes as if his brain might have just switched on. Salerno thought for a moment and then said, "I was thinking about joining. I was working out down at the BAC but this is closer to Sal's house."

"It's a nice place, they keep it pretty clean. And the New Year's Resolution crowd is starting to thin out."

The kid must have missed the reference to the January rush that always follows the holidays because he looked dumbfounded. Tom wondered if the kid knew anymore than Sal had let on. He went on, "Oh and you'll have to excuse my uncle the other day. He can be a real hard ass."

Salerno shrugged. "Don't worry about it. Sal can be an aggravating old prick himself."

"I could see why he would want to wash his hands of Little Mike though."

Another shrug and Salerno said, "Eh, the old man doesn't have the stomach for that kind of stuff any more. Besides Mike is fucking crazy, running around with a missing finger like it's some kind of badge of honor."

An alarm went off in Tom's head but he kept up the banter. "Yeah I heard he was a bad ass from way back."

Salerno got quiet for a moment and then looked uncomfortable again. Tom didn't want to push his luck. "Well I better get going," he said. "I just came out to grab my sneakers."

"Okay, take it easy."

As Tom went towards his car he glanced over his shoulder and sure enough, Salerno was going inside the gym. At least he was going to make it look good. He changed his footwear and went back inside and climbed onto an elliptical machine. He chose one where he could watch the front desk where Salerno was filling out a membership application. After a minute Salerno looked up and spoke to Anna, the girl working the counter. She said something to him and he picked up the application and walked out the door. Before he made the entrance Salerno shot a glance across the gym floor. Tom pretended he was watching one of the televisions mounted on the wall when Salerno looked his way. As soon as he went outside Tom hopped off the machine and went to the doorway just in time to see Salerno getting into a late model, red Ford Mustang. Tom went back to the desk and got Anna's attention.

"Hey, I think I know that guy who was just up here. Did he join the gym?"

Anna was pulling her long brown hair back into a ponytail and shook her head. "No, he started to fill out the application but took it with him. He said he forgot his wallet."

"Oh."

"He looked like he could stand to do some cardio."

Tom smiled and said, "Why is that?"

Anna smiled back. "His face was flushed and he was sweating like a pig just from the walk in from the parking lot."

Tom went back to resume his workout although his mind wasn't on it anymore. Sal Manzella had said he hadn't seen Mike in over a year. The fact that Salerno, Sal's houseboy by proxy, knew about the missing finger made Tom wonder if that was true.

He finished his workout and headed back to the apartment. He now had a few stops to make that night.

Chapter 19

Tom went home and took a shower. He thought about calling his uncle and telling him about running into Mark Salerno, but decided to keep that to himself for a while. He killed some time watching the news and reading the paper and then at 7:00 PM he headed out.

He did a slow drive-by at the Son's of Eire then turned around and parked on the other side of the street. He was far enough away from the building to be inconspicuous, while still being able to see the Club's parking lot as well as the front entrance. It was still light out so he didn't dare get any closer.

When he arrived there was only one car in the lot, parked towards the rear. Then a few people started to drift in; first Dominic the bartender, probably reporting for his shift, rode up on a bike and went in the side entrance. Then a few men, probably members, entered the front entrance. After an hour, he was just starting to wonder if he was wasting his time when the side door opened and two men emerged.

Twilight was spreading out and the parking lot's lights had yet to kick on but Tom recognized them; it was the guitar player, Seamus McNally and the man he had gotten into a fight with the last time he had visited.

McNally was carrying a guitar case and seemed to be in a heated conversation with the second man. He put the case into the back seat of a car and turned and said something to the second man. The second man threw up his hands and said something in return and then the McNally shook his head, climbed in the car and started it.

Tom remembered McNally's reaction the first time they had seen each other. That seemed to have triggered Tom's hasty ejection from the Club. What had caused McNally's reaction?

McNally pulled out of the lot and headed north on Abbott Road. Tom made sure the other man had gone back into the Club and then pulled out to follow. McNally worked his way over to South Ogden Street and then onto I-190. The traffic picked up there so Tom was able to get closer while still leaving a couple of cars in between himself and the silver Pontiac McNally was driving. McNally exited onto I-90 and headed east. Twenty minutes later McNally exited the thruway at Niagara Falls Boulevard and Tom knew where he was probably heading. He let up off the gas and gave his quarry some more space.

Molly's Pub sat on a lot on the Boulevard that had been an RV dealership for years. The pub had relocated from a smaller place in Cheektowaga after their lease ran out and it was sold to the Airport for parking spaces. The pub was already established before the move as a bit of Ireland in the suburbs and the crowd followed along to their new larger digs. Live Irish music on the weekends, dart leagues during the week and an honest pint of Guinness all week long.

Tom cruised the lot and spotted McNally's car. He waited a few minutes and then went inside. The hostess station by the front door was abandoned. There was a dining room off to the right and the pub itself sat off to the left. Tom lingered by the door and scanned the pub. McNally was already on the stage at the back of the room, by himself, tuning his guitar with a pint of stout on the stool next to him. The bar ran along most of the left side of the room. Tom went to the end farthest away from the stage and settled in.

He ordered a Harp from the bartender and looked around the room. There were about thirty people at the bar and the small tables scattered around. The stage was well lit so he had little apprehension about McNally spotting him. After a few minutes McNally introduced himself to polite applause. He launched into a set of traditional Irish folk music.

He hadn't heard live Irish music since he was fourteen years old. His father had brought him down to the bar on St. Patrick's Day to help out with the dishes and stocking the bar. A little after midnight Tom and another kid, Bill Kirnen had smuggled a couple of beers out the back door and were drinking them in the chill March air out by the dumpster when his father caught them. Tom remembered standing slack-jawed while his father stared daggers at him.

"What the hell do you think you're doing?" his father finally spoke.

"It's just a beer," Tom replied meekly.

His father walked over, snatched the bottles from them and poured them out. "Do you know how many cops are in there tonight?"

Tom found being scolded in front of his friend, whom he was trying to impress, embarrassing. He grew defiant. "Technically, I'm not even supposed to be working here," he said. "And Jesus Dad, it was just one beer."

Big Tom glared at his son for a moment and then looked at Bill Kirnen. "Billy, you're all done for tonight. Come back tomorrow and see Mr. Brennan to get paid."

Without a word Bill turned on his heel and fled into the night, leaving Tom alone with his father.

"You're fourteen years old," his father began. "Do you want to end up like all of those rummies in the bar?"

Tom looked down, angry, embarrassed and ashamed.

Big Tom went on, "Do you want to be a boxer or not?"

"Yeah but—"

Big Tom stepped right in front of him and put a finger in his face. "Half the guys I went to high school with spend most of their paychecks on getting tight. Then there are the ones who can't keep a job because they're shit-faced all the time. They're bad at everything; marriage, parenting, hell, life in general, with the exception of getting drunk. I know it's just a beer, but you're way too young to be starting down that path. Wait 'til you do something with your life before you go there."

Tom looked up at his dad and said, "Sorry."

"Not as sorry as you'll be if your mother finds out. She didn't even want me to bring you down here today." His father turned to go in but then remembered something. He faced Tom again. "Oh, and this will tie in with today's lesson. Some drunk just got sick all over the men's room. Grandpa wants it cleaned up."

Tom didn't have a drink again until he was a freshman in college.

His cell phone buzzed in his pocket snapping him out of his reverie. He took it out and looked at the caller ID. It was a number he thought he recognized so he stepped over to the hostess stand and answered it.

"Tommy?" A familiar voice said.

"Whitey?"

"The same," Brennan responded.

"What can I do for you?"

"Tommy, I need you to do me a favor."

"What's that?"

"I'm outside in the parking lot. I need you to come out right now."

What the hell? Tom thought. "Whitey, I'm actually on a job right now."

"Don't bullshit me son, I know what you're doing. Now get out here before I have to come in there and drag your ass out."

Tom glanced up at the stage. McNally was warbling his way through "The Green, Green Grass of Home." He had a fresh pint on the stool next to him and didn't look like he was going anywhere. "I'll be right out."

As soon as Tom stepped out of the door Whitey edged up in his Cadillac. He leaned over and opened the passenger side door. Without a word he drove to the rear of the lot and stopped in front of Tom's car.

"What the fuck are you doing?" Tom asked thoroughly confused.

"Go home Tommy," Whitey said putting his car in park.

"Let me ask you a couple of questions first," Tom said, his blood rising.

Whitey exhaled and frowned. "What?" he said.

"How..." Where to start? Tom thought. "How did you know I was here? And how do you know what I'm doing? And why do I have to leave?"

"Tom, your granddad..." Whitey sputtered.

"Fuck granddad," Tom exploded. "Since when do I answer to him?"

Whitey glared at Tom and said, "First of all, watch your mouth, you impertinent little shit. Secondly, do you know who you're messing around with?" He gestured back towards the pub.

I've got a pretty good idea."

"Do you?" Whitey asked incredulously.

"What do you mean?"

Whitey gritted his teeth and said, "It's the fucking IRA. Fucking terrorists."

Tom sat back and looked at his friend. "I heard a rumor."

"Well, it's not just a rumor. They're the real fucking deal. Did you know you were followed here tonight?"

Salerno, Tom thought. "A red Mustang?"

Whitey furrowed his brow and said, "Yeah, did you see it?"

"Ah... that's somebody else," Tom said.

"Damn it Tom, what else have you gotten yourself into?"

"Don't worry about that now. How do you know that these guys are in the IRA?"

Whitey looked at his steering wheel and thought for a moment. He seemed to be thinking about what to say next. Finally he said, "This goes back to when your father died... Hugh knows who they are."

Tom felt his face get hot. "They killed my father? Why didn't Hugh say anything?"

Whitey shook his head. "He had his reasons Tom." He hesitated and then, "Look, I've already said too much. Hugh wants you to drop this."

"Tell him thanks, but fuck off."

Whitey's expression turned grave. "He said he's going to handle it."

Tom put his hand on the door latch and said, "He's had twenty three years to handle it. It's my turn now." And with that he opened the door and jumped out. As he slammed it shut he heard Whitey call his name.

Tom went back into the pub. He had to will his heart rate back to normal and try to remember that he wanted to blend in. McNally was on a break and standing at the end of the bar near the stage talking to the bartender. After about ten minutes he went back up on stage with another pint and started up. He was slurring his words and his playing was sloppy, but he soldiered on. About midnight the crowd started to thin out and Tom took one last look around the room, saw no one that caught his interest and decided to wait for McNally outside.

At 12:45 AM McNally walked unsteadily to his car and started back towards the city. Tom had half a mind to call the Tonawanda police and report an erratic driver but decided that he didn't want McNally knocked off his routine. He followed him into South Buffalo to a small apartment off of Tifft Street and watched him stagger inside, banging his guitar case on the doorway as he entered.

It was hard to believe the guy was a freedom fighter/terrorist. He looked like some drunken Irish expatriate cashing in on being a marginally talented musician catering to some suburbanites love of all things Irish. Still, Tom knew his grandfather had been holding something back for all these years. And the old man had never been shy about demanding a pound of flesh if he had been crossed. Hugh's own son had probably been murdered and he hadn't reacted. There had to have been some kind of leverage, a threat perhaps that would make the old man act so out of character.

Chapter 20

Before he left McNally at home to sleep it off Tom got out of his car and scanned the street for signs of life. Salerno obviously wasn't the brightest bulb, using a cherry red Mustang for a surveillance car. He didn't see any signs of his tail so he hopped back into the Chevy and pulled away from the curb.

Why would Sal Manzella have his house boy following him? Then there was Salerno's quasi admission that he had seen Mike Manzella recently enough to know about the missing finger. That could hypothetically mean that Sal had seen him too and had lied about it. Tom decided to make one more stop before going home.

Thirty minutes later Tom pulled up across the street from Sal Manzella's house on Saranac Avenue. The house was pitch black so Tom retrieved the Mag light he kept in the glove compartment and slipped out the door. It was after two a.m. so the street was deserted with only the sound of light traffic one block away on Hertel Avenue.

He walked across the street and up the driveway. There didn't seem to be a light on in the entire house. He crept back to the detached garage and shined his light into the window. It was a single car structure and in the dim light he saw Sals Manzella's Lincoln but no Mustang or other car that would imply that someone else was in the house. Tom walked up to the back door and peered into the darkness of what appeared to be the kitchen. He fished the flashlight out of his pocket and aimed it through the window. Most of the light just reflected off the glass but Tom saw something on the floor in the doorway leading out of the kitchen.

It was a pair of feet with what looked like slippers on them. He changed the angle of the light and made out Sal Manzella laying on his back half way out of the kitchen into the dining room. Tom tried to see if Manzella was breathing but couldn't be sure through the bad lighting.

He thought briefly about calling 911 but his curiosity got the better of him and he picked up a ceramic garden gnome off the bottom step and used it to knock out the bottom pane of glass. He reached and unlocked the dead bolt and let himself in. He flipped on the light switch and hurried over to Sal to check for a pulse. As soon as he bent over the old man he knew it was too late. Sal's already pale skin was now completely gray and there was a bullet hole in his forehead. His brown eyes stared vacantly out into nothing.

"Shit," Tom said out loud. He took out his phone and walked back out the door and dialed the number for emergency services. As he reached the bottom of the back stairs a bright light blinded him. He put his hand on his belt but of course, there was no weapon there.

"Police, Let me see your hands!" came a young voice from behind the light.

Tom obliged immediately because the kid sounded like he was all adrenaline.

"There's a body in the kitchen," Tom offered by way of an explanation.

"Hold still," the young patrolman replied. And then he keyed the radio microphone on his shoulder. "I've got a guy in back matching the description. Just came out the door. Looks like some broken glass."

"This isn't what it looks like," Tom said.

He heard footsteps coming up the driveway and then another, older cop came around the corner with his gun out but lowered.

"Get against the wall." The first cop said. Tom was cuffed and read his Miranda rights. As he was being lead down the driveway two more cruisers showed up and then an EMT truck. He knew as soon as they figured out who he was his uncle Sam would be getting a call. He was already dreading the lecture and cursing himself for getting involved in another mess. He wasn't worried about the body. Obviously a neighbor had called about a possible prowler and the cops would find that Sal Manzella had been dead for hours. He had broken in though and would have to explain himself. The worst part was that it happened in his uncle's precinct.

They arrived at D district headquarters on Hertel Avenue and Tom had his keys, watch, wallet and cell phone taken away. To his surprise he wasn't booked or fingerprinted. He recognized a few of the cops he had worked with while he was on the job but most of them seemed to avoid making eye contact. He was put into an interrogation room and the handcuffs were removed. There was a video camera up in the corner of the sparse, cold room with a red light shining steadily, he was being watched.

He wasn't sure how much time had passed when the door swung open and in walked Detective James Foster with a uniformed officer. Foster took a seat across the metal table from Tom and the uniform stayed by the door with his arms folded across his chest.

Tom was wondering if things could possibly get worse. The detective across form him was the same one he had pointed a gun at the previous week. He tried to remain impassive without seeming cocky.

"Anybody you want to call?" Foster asked, looking at Tom with his eyebrows raised.

Tom wasn't sure if Foster was trying to bait him, but he wasn't going to get into it with him. He figured Foster expected him to call his uncle to bail him out again. That was the last person Tom would call, Sam would find out soon enough. He also knew he couldn't afford a lawyer at the moment. "Nope," he said.

"What were you doing at Salvatore Manzella's house?" Foster asked picking up a pen and opening the folder.

"I have reason to believe an associate of his has been following me."

Foster looked up. Apparently he had been expecting Tom to stonewall him. "And why would that be?"

"The associate's name is Mark Salerno. He drives a late model Ford Mustang, New York plates... number 7YA- 2245. I don't know why exactly, but I think it may have something to do with Sal's nephew, Mike."

Foster sat back and scratched his earlobe. "We've been all over Sal this past week," he said. "There's been no sign of Mike Manzella. Now why would you think there is a connection all of a sudden?"

Tom did not want to drop his uncle's name but his narrative needed a little credibility. "I've been told that Sal claimed he hadn't seen Mike in over a year. I ran into Salerno and he let it out that he knew about Mike's missing finger." He raised his left hand and touched his own pinkie with his right hand. "That happened within the last twelve months."

Foster shook his head. "That doesn't connect Sal and Mike. And that doesn't explain why you broke into Sal's house."

Tom had no excuse for that. It had been rash and impulsive. "It's true I overstepped my boundaries. The only reason I went in was I saw Sal on the floor and didn't want to watch him die while I waited on an ambulance."

Foster said, "He'd been dead for at least eight hours."

"It was dark, Foster. I saw the old man lying there and couldn't tell if he was breathing or not."

Foster wrote something else down, closed the file and stood up. Tom read his expression as one of disbelief but he had played it as straight as he dared. Now he was going to have to let it play out.

"We'll be back. Don't go anywhere," Foster said as he turned to leave.

"Are you going to arrest me or what?"

Foster looked back as the patrolman opened the door. "Not yet. But the night is young." The two policemen left the room and Tom heard the door latch behind them.

It was hard to tell how much time passed in the windowless room. Tom got up occasionally to stretch his legs and get his circulation back. He was tired and he realized he hadn't eaten since late yesterday afternoon. Finally the door opened but it wasn't Foster. It was a stocky man with Sergeant's stripes on his uniform. Tom thought he recognized him but it had been a while. His nametag said Sgt. Moretti.

He looked at Tom and crooked his finger. "Tom, come with me," he said.

Tom obliged and stood up and followed Moretti down the hallway past the nearly empty squad room. There was no sign of Foster or the two patrol officers who had brought him in. He thought Moretti might be putting him in the holding cell until he was either released or shipped downtown. It was worse. They stopped in front of a door with a brass plate next to it that said; Captain Dipietro. Moretti knocked twice and opened the door and gestured for Tom to go in.

Tom saw that the sun was coming up through the window behind Sam's desk. Tom knew his uncle had probably come in earlier than usual but there he was, sitting ramrod straight, perfectly groomed and in his usual impeccable uniform. He looked right at Tom and then to Moretti and said, "Thanks, Tony."

Tom didn't sit and Sam didn't tell him to. They just looked at each other for a while.

"I'm not even going to bother asking," Sam finally said. "As a matter of fact, I'm not going to say anything."

Tom didn't reply. He felt like a teenager again, being caught doing something stupid and selfish.

"When this is all done," Sam continued, "I think you should consider what you want to do with the rest of your life. That is, if you don't get yourself killed or thrown in jail.

It may be time for you to relocate."

"Uncle Sam—" Tom started.

"I don't care about my reputation," Sam went on. "I'm four years away from retirement and I'm done sticking my neck out for you. It's your mom. I don't want to have you pissing your life away right in front of her."

The room fell into a static silence. Tom wanted to apologize but knew it would ring hollow. Sam reached for the intercom on his desk and pushed a button. "We're ready Sally," he said into it.

"Foster checked your phone and it showed that you had dialed 911, so your story checked out. Still, it was stupid for you to go in given your history with that family." Sam stood up. "Kid, I'm sorry but this is where I get off."

The door opened behind Tom and he turned around. Special Agent Miller and a two other agents walked in. "Mr. Donovan. We need to talk to you about Brian Dinkle. We would like you to come downtown with us."

Tom supposed he could have turned down Miller's request. What would that accomplish? All Miller would have to do is get a subpoena and then

Tom would have to get a lawyer, which would give the impression he had something to hide. Besides, he knew Miller might have answers to some questions he had.

The two agents with Miller cleared a path and Tom started for the doorway. He couldn't bring himself to look back at his uncle.

Chapter 21

On their way out, Miller led Tom past the booking area where an envelope was passed across the counter to him.

"Sign here," the desk Sergeant said pointing to a clipboard on the counter.

Tom signed the sheet and then opened the envelope. He took out his keys, wallet and watch and was just about to ask the sergeant where his cell phone was when Miller put a hand on his arm.

"We have your phone," Miller said.

Tom turned to face Miller and looked him in the eye. "Don't you need a warrant for that?"

"I could get one in an hour if I have to," Miller said, calling his bluff.

It was a little past seven a.m. when the four men left the station and climbed into a black SUV. It was overcast and cold, more so than it should be in-mid April. Winter seemed to be lingering.

With the morning traffic just starting to pick up, the drive downtown to the FBI's Buffalo office took about twenty minutes. Tom was led to a conference room on the third floor and left with an agent who looked to be in his mid-thirties. Standard Fed attire, dark suit, short hair, serious expression.

After about twenty minutes a group of agents came into the conference room led by Miller. Right behind Miller was a man in his fifties who took a seat at the head of the long table.

Two of the trailing agents set up a video camera, aiming it across the table at a chair that Tom was directed to.

Miller took the seat directly across from Tom and pushed a piece of paper across the table. "Mr. Donovan, you have a right to have counsel present. As this is an informal interview, the document you see in front of you is a consent form to waive that right for this session if you choose to do so."

Tom looked at the document and then glanced around the room. The man at the head of the table was leaning back in his chair looking back at him with an expression that Tom couldn't read. "Informal?" he asked.

"For now," Miller replied, drawing Tom's attention back. "We don't consider you an accomplice of Brian Dinkle's, but we have a few questions regarding your relationship with him and the research he was doing on your behalf."

"Fair enough," Tom said. He signed the document and pushed it back across the table. Miller gave the agent waiting by the video recorder a signal and the agent turned it on.

Miller looked at his watch. "It is Friday, April Nineteen, eight-twenty in the morning. This is a follow up interview with Thomas Donovan. I am Special Agent Patrick Miller. Also present are Agent Nicholas Phelps, Agent Ronald Strauss and Homeland Security Liaison Phillip Marshall." He looked up at Tom and said, "Mr. Donovan, you have agreed to waive your right to counsel at this time?"

"Yes."

The interview lasted for over an hour. Miller asked Tom about what exactly he had asked Brian Dinkle to do, as well as the information that Brian had passed on to Tom. Miller picked up on the thread of Tom's interest in the Sons of Eire Social Club. Tom already knew Brian had made a connection that the FBI was sensitive about. Miller's questions only piqued his curiosity.

Miller also used the old interviewing trick of asking the same question multiple times but each time phrasing it differently. The desired result was either to trip up the interviewee or simply wear him down. Tom had sat on the other side of the table enough times to recognize the game. He kept his answers simple, disclosing nothing that he hadn't told Miller the first time.

He was exhausted and frustrated. He held himself together until Miller asked the question; "How did Mr. Dinkle send you the information in question?"

The MP3 player, Tom thought. There was probably enough there to incriminate Brian, let alone himself.

"Over the series of several phone calls," Tom replied. He willed himself to maintain eye contact and not give anything away.

Miller circled back to the Sons Of Eire. "What was the purpose of your visit to the social club last week?"

"I was thinking of joining. I'm half Irish."

Marshall, the middle aged man from Homeland Security let out a snort. Out of the corner of his eye Tom could see him scowling.

Miller was growing agitated. "Mr. Donovan, I don't think you appreciate the gravity of this situation. Mr. Dinkle will be prosecuted under the Computer Fraud and Abuse Act and will do time in federal prison. Any associate found to be complicit in his illegal activities will face the same."

"Sounds good," Tom said. "Then maybe while we're clearing the air you can explain why the FBI covered up a possible homicide involving someone associated with the Sons of Eire in 1989? Oh, and who exactly is Mr. Jones?"

Miller sat with his mouth open. Marshall brought the palm of his hand down audibly on the table and said, "Turn it off."

The agent near the recorder took a few seconds and then realized Marshall was speaking to him. He fumbled for the button and then powered it off. Marshall stood up and looked at Miller and said, "Pat, come with me."

Marshall stalked out of the room with Miller at his heel. Tom leaned back in his chair and exhaled then noticed the agent by the video recorder looking at him with a confused expression.

"Must have been something I said," Tom offered.

The agent frowned and then the door opened up and Miller said something to the man standing by the door and then disappeared.

The agent walked over to Tom and said, "Get up."

Tom was taken down to the basement and placed in a small windowless holding room with only a bench running along one side of it. He remembered reading about the Computer Fraud and Abuse Act and how it had been attached to the Patriot Act. The fact that Homeland Security was involved meant that Brian Dinkle and he were indeed in deep shit.

He sat on the bench. There was no telling how long he would be here. The Feds might be ransacking his apartment at that very moment. If they were using the Patriot Act, the government could use extraordinary measures to get what they were after.

In his mind he went over what he had told Miller. He hadn't been completely forthcoming, especially about the files Brian had sent on the MP3 player, but he hadn't technically lied either. What was done, was done for the time being. A wave of fatigue was washing over him. He stretched out on the bench and closed his eyes. Without intending to he soon fell fast asleep.

Probably because he knew he couldn't go anywhere or do anything Tom let his mind shut down and slept soundly. If he dreamed at all he wouldn't remember it. He was so out of it that it took him a few seconds to remember where he was when Agent Miller finally shook him out of his stupor.

"Donovan! Jesus Christ, I thought you were dead."

Tom sat up slowly as he regained his wits. "Not yet," he said.

Miller stepped back and looked down at him. "We're going to give you one more chance," he said.

Tom worked a kink out of his neck. "Chance to do what?"

"Play ball. All we want is Dinkle."

Tom shook his head and said, "I told you everything-"

Miller cut him off. "Bullshit. I know you probably don't know where he is but I've got a good idea you can help us find him."

"And even if I could, why would I do that?"

Miller tried to look menacing now and was doing a pretty good job with his bulk and his crooked nose. He took a step towards Tom and put a finger in his face. "If you don't we are going to crawl so far up your ass you'll be able to taste it."

Tom glared past the finger and into Miller's eyes. "This is bullshit!" he said.

Miller dropped the finger and said, "What's bullshit is that your pal Dinkle has hacked into federal government files and drawn the attention of Homeland Security. They give the go ahead and we can make things very unpleasant."

Tom wondered just how much more unpleasant things could get for him. Miller pressed on. "We can pull your PI license, shut down Frederickson and Associates and make sure Ms. Palkowski gets bounced out of the Police Academy before she even starts."

Tom felt like he had been punched in the stomach. Miller, and the people he worked for, were dead serious. He hated being backed into a corner. He thought for a minute while Miller continued to glare at him and then realized somebody was going to have to get screwed over.

"Okay," he said. "I can contact Dinkle. But I can't do it from here."

Miller furrowed his brow and folded his thick arms across his chest. His answer would tell Tom a thing or two.

"Okay, I'll have a guy take you to your car. You have twenty-four hours to help us get a line on him. All we need is a trail, an IP address would be a good start." Miller stepped back again and gestured to the door.

"Got it." Tom knew that if Miller accepted the terms he proposed that meant that his phone and his computer had most likely been tapped.

"Oh and Donovan, don't even think about trying to fuck me over or everything I told you before will come true and then some."

"Got it."

Tom was dropped off at his car at 6:35 PM. He climbed in and waited until the agent who dropped him off was out of sight and then he got back out and popped the trunk. At the bottom of his gym bag he found the MP3 player. If the Feds had searched his car they either didn't want to rummage through his dirty socks or had missed it. He tried to turn on his cell phone but the battery was dead. The AC adaptor in his car was broken, rendering his car charger useless. He raced back to his apartment.

As soon as he was inside he turned on his laptop and logged onto his email. He powered up the MP3 player and found the file that Brian had sent him. At the very end there was an address for a Hotmail account with a note next to it that said, "Use on emergency only."

Tom wrote an email that said:

Couple of questions about the S.O.E. Give me a call when you can.

He retrieved his phone charger from the bedroom and plugged it in. He had missed six calls while his phone had been held by the cops and then the Feds. There was only one voicemail and Tom was just about to check it when the phone buzzed in his hand. The caller ID said, *"Restricted."*

"Major Tom," Brian Dinkle said as soon as Tom answered.

"Hey Brian, thanks for calling back. I'd ask you how the weather was but you probably wouldn't tell me."

Brian chuckled and said, "You've got that right. The less you know the better. Oh, and I guess I left a bit of a mess there, didn't I?"

"I wouldn't use Cal for a job reference if I were you. The Feds were at the office asking questions but I don't think they have much."

"How about you Tommy? How are things going otherwise?"

"Tell you the truth Bri', I've had quite the run of bad luck this week."

There was brief pause and then Brian came back; "What can I do for you?"

"Just wondering if you had anything else on Mr. Jones or the Sons of Eire?"

"I do have something that might interest you," Brian said. "You don't think your computer is tapped do you?"

"I doubt it. They didn't seem too interested in what I had to say."

Tom heard Brian pecking away at his keyboard and then Brian said, "Okay, I just sent you something. Check your inbox in a second."

Tom opened up his e-mail and sure enough there was a new message from a different address. "Got it. Thanks Brian."

"Anything else?"

"No, I'll look this over."

"It's been a pleasure as always Major Tom."

"Same here. Take care of yourself Brian."

The line went dead. Tom took out Miller's business card and punched in the number. Miller answered on the second ring.

"Did you get it?" Tom said in lieu of hello.

"Get what?" Miller asked.

"Cut the crap Miller. I know my phone and computer are tapped. Did you get the e-mail from Dinkle?"

Miller hesitated and then said, "Yeah."

"Okay, I did my part now you need to keep up your end of the deal."

"You haven't given us shit yet Donovan."

Tom raised his voice, "You said all you needed was an IP address. I gave you that and a cell phone to trace. I have had enough of your

'Weight of the Federal Government' bullshit so you can either tell me about the Sons of Eire or my next call will be to my lawyer and the ACLU."

"Take it easy tough guy," Miller said sternly. "Alright. You want to know about Mr. Jones? I'll tell you, but you'd better be careful with what you do with what I tell you."

"Go ahead."

"The man you know as Seamus McNally is actually named Gerry O'Connor, AKA Mr. Jones. He was in the witness protection program."

Tom was incredulous. "You had some psycho bomb-thrower in witness protection?"

"I don't know where you got that information from Donovan but it's bullshit."

"What do you mean?"

"Listen, I'll send you a copy of his file, but like I said, don't do anything stupid."

"Do it," Tom said. "You already have my e-mail address."

"Whatever," Miller said and then hung up.

Tom had no sooner set his phone down when it buzzed again. He looked at the caller ID and it was a local number that he thought he had seen before.

"Hello?"

"Tom, it's Grace. Did you get my message?"

Tom was flustered. "I just got my phone back..."

"Back from-" Grace cut herself off. "Alicia Simmons' mother called for you. She said that there has been a car driving by the house for the last couple of hours and the police dispatcher told them they would send a car but then nobody came."

Alicia Simmons was the girl who had been put into the hospital by members of the NBH, an East side street gang headed by Derrick "Terror" Trent, a man Tom later shot and killed in the incident that led to the end of his time as a policeman. Alicia had testified on Tom's behalf at his Grand Jury trial and he had stayed in touch with the family.

"When was this?" Tom said standing up.

"About an hour ago. We couldn't get a hold of you so Cal went over there."

"What?"

"Tom, I'm worried. He's been gone for an hour and now he won't answer his phone."

Shit, Tom thought. "Grace, do me a favor. Call the Cheektowaga police and-"

"Cheektowaga?" Grace interrupted.

"Yeah, the Simmons' moved a couple of months ago. Didn't they tell Cal?"

There was silence and then Tom heard Grace swallow and say, "Tom he went to the house on Krupp Avenue."

Chapter 22

Krupp Avenue was located on Buffalo's East side, an area Tom Donovan was familiar with, having spent the better part of his ten years as a cop patrolling its hard luck neighborhoods. Originally populated by Polish and German immigrants during the city's early and mid-twentieth century boom, it had fallen on hard times after the bottom fell out of the area's manufacturing sector and the growth of the first-ring suburbs. Real estate prices plummeted, many of the neighborhood churches closed their doors and bars, markets and businesses were all shuttered. Given all that, there was still an element of good that Tom saw amidst the poverty and the crime. There were people down there just trying to live their lives the right way, even trying to better themselves, despite the odds. One of those people was Alicia Simmons, an honor student and a person who had the audacity to speak up against the criminal element in the neighborhood in an attempt to protect her brother.

Tom raced down Bailey Avenue and then cut off two cars coming the other way when he made a left onto Broadway. A light, cold rain was falling from the darkened sky. He turned left onto Krupp and his heart sank.

There were flashing lights everywhere. He double parked his car on the right side of the street and got out. Tom could see beyond the cruisers that the Simmons' former front yard had been cordoned off with yellow police tape. In the driveway he saw Cal Frederickson's silver Acura parked with the door open and a crime scene technician leaning into it. He started in that direction but came face to face with a young female officer.

"Sir, I'm going to have to ask you to stay back."

Tom kept moving forward until she put a hand on his chest. He finally realized she was talking to him. "What happened?" he asked.

"It's a crime scene, sir," she said.

"I can see that! What happened?"

"Donovan!" A voice came from the side. Tom looked over and saw Sergeant David Beverly, with whom he had worked for several years walking towards him.

Tom stepped back and the female officer withdrew her hand, seemingly relieved that she didn't have to deal with this deranged man herself.

"Dave, what happened?" Tom knew that Beverly was familiar with his history with the Simmons family and hoped he would give him a straight answer.

Beverly put a hand on Tom's arm and led him away from the perimeter. Tom resisted slightly but then gave in.

Beverly, satisfied that he was out of the other policeman's earshot looked Tom in the eye and asked, "You work for Cal Frederickson, don't you?"

"You know I do Dave. Where is he?"

"What are you doing here Tom?"

"Cal's wife called me. She said that Alicia Simmons was scared about something. They couldn't find me so Cal came down."

Beverly's expression turned grim and he broke eye contact.

"Dave, where is he?"

Just then an ambulance pulled away slowly, lights on, no siren.

"He's dead Tom. Shot three times at close range."

Tom looked down at the ground and lost all the feeling in his body, he couldn't feel the rain or the cold or sense the people around him, just the shock and sorrow for the man who had been shot down by bullets intended for him.

Chapter 23

Tom didn't know how long he stood there with his head down. His emotions were careening between shock, guilt and a building rage that he felt for the man who killed his boss. It had to be Manzella. The NBH, having learned that Derrick Trent was turning informer for the DEA two years ago had circled the wagons and gone underground. The immediate threat to the Simmons family was thought to have lessened, most of the scores that Trent felt he had to settle died with him in the McKinley Projects three years earlier. Nevertheless, the Simmons had fled the sight of so much of their misery and moved away from Krupp Avenue as soon as they had the chance. Besides, the trap had been intended for him; it had to be Manzella.

"Tom." It was Sgt. Beverly again, snapping him out of his trance. Standing next to him was Detective Paul Alessi. Tom had worked with Alessi for a brief period on the BPD's gang task force.

Tom looked at the two men and tried to focus on the present.

Alessi was about Tom's age but looked older. The hair at his temples was turning gray and he carried about twenty extra pounds. He looked at Tom with piercing blue eyes.

"Tom," he started. "I'm sorry about Cal."

"Are you the lead?" Tom asked.

"No, they called in Homicide for this one. It's Chuck Falcone."

Tom knew of Falcone by reputation only. He was one of the best. His methods were sometimes unorthodox and he had a bit of an ego, but his clearance rate was the pride of the Homicide division.

"We're going to need a statement," Alessi said.

Tom didn't want to spend another night in a police station but he knew he had to go in. His boss, the man who had taken a chance on him and put up with his impulsive behavior was dead and he had to give the cops anything he could to help them.

"Are you okay to drive?" Beverly asked.

The question didn't register with Tom at first and then he came to. He was more than willing to help the investigation but he wanted access to his car as soon as he had fulfilled that obligation.

"Yeah, let's go."

Alessi took Tom into an interview room at the station on Bailey. Tom held nothing back. He told him that he doubted that it was the NBH. Alessi agreed with him and added that the gang had their hands too full right now with the police and two of the rival gangs in the area to be worried about a three year old grudge started by a turncoat.

Tom told him about his run-in with Manzella as well as the threats he made. Alessi seemed incredulous at first but Tom told him about Manzella's out of town connections as well as being followed by Mark Salerno. He also threw in that he suspected that Manzella had killed his own uncle Sal and that he was capable of anything.

"Alright. Thank you Mr. Donovan. We may be contacting you for a follow-up interview." With that Alessi turned off the recorder on the table and sat back in his chair.

"Jesus Christ, Tom," Alessi said.

"I know."

"Off the record, is there anything else you think might be relevant here?"

Tom frowned. "Like what?"

Alessi picked up on Tom's tone and said, "Tom, I'm not the enemy here. I just want to make sure that we've got everything so we can get this fuck."

"Sorry Paul. Manzella threatened my family and now he killed my friend. I just told you everything I know."

The two men fell silent for a moment. Then Tom's curiosity got the better of him. "Paul, what happened?"

Alessi looked thoughtfully at the pen in his hand. Finally, he looked up and said, "Looks like he got it on his way up the front walk. The shooter stepped out around the corner of the house and opened fire before Cal could draw his weapon."

Tom could see only red. Alessi went on; "Cal had a forty-five on him in a shoulder holster but never had a chance to pull it."

"Who called it in?"

"The old lady next door. She was terrified. She was there when the thing with Alicia Simmons went down too. But you know how it is down here Tom; either nobody saw anything or they're too scared to look out their windows when the shooting starts."

"And the bogus call to the agency?" Tom asked.

"We have a warrant for the phone records Tom. You know we're looking at everything."

Tom realized there was nothing more to be accomplished here and now all he wanted to do was get out of the claustrophobic room he was in as well as the police station.

"I know. Thanks Paul."

Alessi thought for a moment and then asked, "You got a piece Tom?"

Tom cringed on the inside and then said, "Yeah, I got my permit a couple of weeks ago."

Alessi stood up and extended his hand. "You be careful until we find this prick, alright?"

Tom had a panicked thought. "Shit. Grace... has anybody told his wife?"

"It's been taken care of Tom."

As Tom walked out of the station he pulled out his phone and called the number Grace had called him from. It rang six times and then went to her voicemail. He found his car where he had parked on a side street next to the station and climbed in, put the key in the ignition and then his hands fell into his lap. He closed his eyes tightly but then opened them up just in time to see a shadow pass by his window. His heart skipped a beat and then he saw it was a kid, no older than twelve or thirteen, looking back at him giving him the stink eye. Tom stared the kid down for a second until he walked past.

His phone buzzed and he realized he was still holding it in his left hand. It was Sherry.

"Where are you?" She said.

"At the station on Bailey. I just gave a statement."

"Meet me at your place."

"I have something I need to do," Tom said flatly.

"Tom, just do me a favor and come to your apartment first." She was pleading and sounded genuinely upset.

"Okay, I'll be there in fifteen."

Chapter 24

Tom thought about calling his Grandfather's bar and asking Whitey Brennan to get him a gun but remembered that his phone was in all likelihood tapped and didn't want anything else to slow him down. Not that he had a plan at the moment but he wanted to be able to move about as freely and with as little scrutiny from the Feds as possible. He was still too angry to think straight and knew he had to slow down and consider his next step.

As he pulled into a spot near his apartment Sherry popped out of her Toyota Camry from the other side of the street and walked quickly over to him. The street was dark and it wasn't until she had gotten close to him that he could see that her eyes were red from crying.

"Are you okay?" she asked.

"No, I'm not. Come on let's go inside."

They trudged upstairs and Tom opened the door and then glanced out the front window to the street, nothing moving.

Tom plopped down on his recliner and Sherry sat down on the old couch across from him. Her black raincoat opened revealing her Sig Sauer .45 in a cross draw holster. He looked up from the gun to her face just as a single tear rolled down her cheek. Tom had never seen her get emotional before, and thinking he was the cause of it affected him profoundly.

"I'm sorry," he said quietly.

Sherry wiped the tear and shook her head. "You didn't shoot him.

"It was supposed to be me."

"I should have gone with him."

"What do you mean?" Tom asked.

"I was at the office when the call came in and offered to go. He pulled his macho paternal bullshit and said it was probably nothing and told me to go home..." her voice trailed off.

It was obvious that she wanted to say or ask something but couldn't bring herself to do it. Tom had seen the look before. He took a guess as to what it was.

"I was in a holding room at the FBI building all day. They had my phone and when I got it back it was dead."

She furrowed her brow and asked, "The FBI?" And then, "About Brian?"

"Yep."

Tom brought it back to the matter at hand. "I don't think it was the NBH."

This got her attention and she looked up at Tom. "What? Who was it?"

"Manzella," Tom said. "He's gone off the rails. I think he killed his uncle too."

Sherry frowned, confused. "But the call from Alicia's mother?"

Tom got up and went back to the window. "It was bullshit. The Simmons moved out of that house months ago. The cops are probably tracing the call right now."

They fell quiet and the static in the room hung over them. Tom was restless and walked towards the kitchen. "Do you want anything?" he asked.

Sherry put her head back against the wall and said, "Water."

Tom came back with a bottle of water for Sherry and a beer for himself. His head was pounding again. He didn't know if it was just stress or some residual effect of the concussion. Sherry had taken her coat and the holster off and placed them on the coffee table in front of the couch and put her feet up. She seemed to be studying Tom through half closed eyes.

"Where's your Glock?" she asked.

The question hit him like another blow to his skull. He realized he hadn't told anyone about the theft. He sat down again and put his head in his hands and rubbed his temples. "Somebody broke in and took it," he said.

Sherry sat up with her eyes wide open. "Shit, Tom. When?"

He was embarrassed and angry and he snapped, "A couple of days ago."

Sherry was taken aback by his tone and then her face softened. "Well, that settles it then."

Tom felt himself blushing, now more embarrassed by his outburst than anything. "Settles what?" he asked.

She stretched back out on the couch again. "I'm going to camp out here until they find the fucker who shot Cal."

"Sherry, you don't have to—"

"I'm not leaving," she interrupted. "I'm not going to lose you too. Not tonight."

"What about Amber?" he asked, referring to her domestic partner.

"She's out of town at an art show. Nope, Donovan, you and me are going to stick together tonight."

Tom didn't really want a babysitter but knew Sherry could be as stubborn as he was.

"You weren't planning on going anywhere tonight anyway? Were you?" She asked.

"No," he lied. "If you're going to stay you may as well take the bed."

She rolled onto her side and looked at him. "Right, and let you sneak out and do something crazy? She knew him too well.

"I'll get you a blanket."

Chapter 25

Another restless night. When Tom did nod off he would be awakened by disturbing dreams or imagined noises. At about four a.m., on his way to the bathroom he looked into the living room. In the dim light coming from the streetlight outside he saw Sherry stir and look at him.

"What?" she asked, sounding like she was wide awake.

"Nothing. Sorry, go back to sleep."

Back in his bed he eventually drifted off into a fitful sleep until he heard his doorbell ring. He looked at the clock on his nightstand, it was 7:10 AM. He leapt out of bed and went to the front door but Sherry had already gone downstairs to answer it. He was worried until he heard her talking to someone at the front door. When he came around the landing he saw her talking to a man through the barely opened door. She had her gun in her right hand behind her back.

"Who is it Sher'?"

She opened the door all the way and in stepped Detective Chuck Falcone. Falcone looked at Sherry and then at Tom and said, "Nice security system you got here Tommy."

They went backup stairs and into the living room. Tom offered to make coffee.

"Nah, I'm good," the detective said. He was in his fifties with hair that was still black and a heavy set frame. His suit jacket was starting to show signs of strain and the top button on his shirt was undone with his tie pulled down a good three inches. "I already talked to Paul Alessi about your statement. I just wanted to follow up on a few things."

"Go ahead."

"We're going on the theory that it was Manzella," Falcone went on. "The call came from a cell phone in The Falls. Of course it was a prepaid phone."

"The Falls?" Sherry asked.

"We're pretty sure that's where Manzella's been holed up since he attacked you," he said looking from Sherry to Tom. "He still has a couple of cousins in the mob up there, and they may be sympathetic. More so than his family in Buffalo."

"Like his uncle?" Tom offered.

"Precisely. We went through the uncle's house and found some floor boards pulled up in a closet upstairs. The kind of place where the old man would likely have stashed some money. I wouldn't put it past Manzella to ice his own family if he was hard up for cash."

Tom just looked at Falcone not knowing what to say. So far there hadn't been anything that resembled a question.

"I need full disclosure Tom," Falcone pressed on. "From the beginning. Tell me about Manzella, the uncle, Mark Salerno. I know you gave Alessi a lot of it last night, but I want to make sure we didn't miss anything."

Tom sighed and said, "Alright, but you may want to sit down; this is going to take a while."

"I'll make the coffee," Sherry said and headed for the kitchen.

Tom told Falcone just about everything, from Manzella singling him out for revenge to his uncle Sam confronting Sal Manzella and his encounters with Mark Salerno. He also offered the theory that Salerno was probably the one who knew where Sal kept his money and passed that information on to Mike Manzella. He didn't know what kind of hold Mike had over Salerno, but it probably had something to do with Sal treating Salerno like his house boy. Falcone interrupted a few times to ask questions and take notes.

Falcone was looking at his notebook and chewing on the end of his pen. He suddenly looked Tom right in the eye and asked, "So why is Mike Manzella so sure that you were the one who made a mess of his business last year?"

Tom didn't hesitate. "Because I did it." Out of the corner of his eye he could see Sherry sit up. Falcone looked at him impassively. Tom continued, "At the end of the Shield's thing I went to the strip club and made it look like a hold up. When the Lackawanna PD showed up they couldn't help but find the drugs that Manzella was selling. Then the whole thing blew up on him. The drugs, the prostitution, the whore house he was running out in Farnham." Sherry went slightly rigid at the mention of 'Farnham.' "All except for one thing."

"What's that?" Falcone asked evenly.

"You have a cold case from last April, Rachel Eberle?"

"Yeah, Henderson caught that one. I know she worked at Showgirls."

"I can't prove it, but I know Manzella did her too."

Falcone looked thoughtful as he scratched his ear lobe with the pen. Finally he looked back up at Tom as he pulled himself up off the couch.

"You know if any of this comes up Tom it's not going to look good," he said.

"I know. But you wanted full disclosure and that's how this all started."

"The paper said that four men took the bar down that night."

"And?" Tom asked.

"And nothing yet," Falcone said as he put his note book into his coat pocket. "If it does come out this won't be pleasant for any of you."

"I understand."

"Oh, and I spoke to your uncle this morning."

Shit, Tom thought, "He has nothing to do with any of this."

Falcone gave Tom a peculiar look. Then he said, "Uh, yeah. I know that. He just told me that you have a habit of acting rashly."

Tom's neck was getting hot. Here it comes, a lecture by proxy.

Falcone went on as he reached for the door, "Just don't do anything crazy OK? And cut your uncle some slack. He's a good guy."

Tom thought for a second and said, "I will."

Falcone turned around once more to face him. "I'm going to do everything I can to find

Manzella or whoever did this. Cal was a good guy too."

"Did you know him?" Sherry asked.

"The first year I was in Homicide he was my partner. Went out of his way to make sure I didn't screw up. Taught me a lot." Falcone looked off, down the stairs and went on, "It still pisses me off about the way he went out."

"What do you mean?" Tom said.

"Fucking Manzella," The detective shook his head. "Our eye witness recanted and the brass came down on Cal. Cal never said it out loud, because he was too proud, but I think we got set up."

Falcone handed Tom a business card and told Tom to call him if he thought of anything else and then he was gone.

Tom and Sherry stood and looked at each other for a moment. And then Tom said, "I've gotta talk to Grace."

Sherry nodded. "I'll go with you."

Tom knew there were things he had to say to Grace that were private but he also knew it would help if he had his friend with him when he did it.

"Do you know where they live?" he asked.

"I know they have a condo by the lake at Harbour Pointe, but I don't know the exact address."

Tom pulled his phone out of his pocket and looked at it. He couldn't bring himself to pull up Grace's number. Sherry seemed to pick up on his hesitation and took her own phone out. "I got it," she said.

Tom started to protest but it was too late and his heart wasn't in it. Sherry found the number and dialed.

"Hello? Grace, it's Sherry... yeah, I'm with Tom and we were wondering if we could come over?"

Sherry stopped and was listening to whatever Grace was saying and then said, "Okay, we'll see you then."

Tom looked at her as she disconnected the call and then turned his palms up in a 'what was that?' gesture.

"She wants us all at the agency in an hour," Sherry answered.

"Shit, I really need a shower," Tom said.

"Me too," Sherry said as she reached for her coat. "I'm going to run home and get changed." She glanced at Tom.

"Don't worry," he said. "I'm not going anywhere else."

Chapter 26

Tom showered and dressed as quickly as possible. He wanted to arrive at the agency ahead of the others so he could speak to Grace privately. When he arrived at the Delaware Avenue office forty minutes later he found that only Simon Willis, the part time retired cop, and Grace were already there. Fortunately, Willis was in his office and on the phone. Tom found Grace in Cal's office seated behind his desk looking through a file.

He knocked lightly on the doorjamb. She looked up at him and he saw the dark circles under her blue eyes. She smiled and said, "Tom, come in." She stood up and walked around the desk. They embraced and then Tom stepped back and started to tear up.

He didn't know where to start. He had tried to think of what to say on his way over but everything he thought of just sounded cliché or hollow. Now he just stood there silently.

Grace put a hand on his cheek and said, "It's alright."

"No it's not Grace. I am so sorry."

She pointed to one of the two chairs in front of Cal's desk and took the other one herself. Tom sat down and looked at his feet. He was close to losing it.

"He knew what he was doing Tom. When Cal retired from the department I thought we were out of the woods, but was I ever mistaken."

He looked up at her.

She went on, "This wasn't the first time since he started this business that he had his life threatened."

"Still, I was the one who was supposed to be there."

Grace brushed some lint off the leg of her black slacks. "Yes, and the only reason you weren't, was because of Brian Dinkle."

"So you know where I was?"

She nodded. "And Cal felt terrible about that. He said that he should have kept closer tabs on Brian. He blamed himself for the trouble that followed."

Tom was in disbelief that Grace could be so forgiving. He knew someday it would give him some comfort, but for now it did little to lessen his guilt. Finally he said, "Are you sure you want to be here today?"

She smiled weakly and said, "I had to get out of the house. Cal's cousin runs a funeral home over on Delavan and he's making all the arrangements. Besides, there's some business to take care of."

Tom looked at her quizzically, wondering what she meant. Just then they heard people entering the outer office. "Hello?" It was Gil Adams.

>>><<<

A few minutes later Grace, Tom, Sherry, Adams and Willis were seated or leaning around Grace's desk in the outer office. The conference room was barely big enough to hold the furniture and equipment in it, let alone five people. Tom glanced around and noticed things were still in a state of disarray from the FBI's intrusion. After Grace answered a few questions about the funeral arrangements she got down to business.

"Before I start, has anyone seen Travis?" She was referring to Cal's nephew and employee.

Everyone shook their heads. "I'm a little concerned. I know Cal's sister told him what happened but I haven't been able to reach him, and I wanted him to be here today."

At first Tom was alarmed. Then the more he thought about it the less worried he became. Travis was a street smart kid. He had been in a gang himself until he witnessed his best friend die in front of him when he was nineteen years old. His uncle Cal had taken him under his wing and given him a job and a direction. Tom just hoped that Travis wasn't doing anything stupid.

Willis spoke up, "I can look for him when we're done here if you want."

"Thank you Simon," Grace said.

Tom was fine with that. He was about to volunteer himself but Willis, like Travis, was black and could go places Tom couldn't without attracting attention. Besides, Tom thought, he had already caused enough damage.

Grace continued, "This is more for Tom, Simon and Gil then, since Sherry is leaving anyway." She hesitated to collect herself. "As you know, even though I know just about every dark corner of my husband's business, Cal is the one who made this thing work." Another pause. The air in the room got a little heavier. "His personality and his connections are what drove the business. He took the jobs that other people wouldn't and he knew the risks." She shot Tom a glance and he almost winced. "That's why he had a contingency plan in place if anything like this ever happened."

Adams spoke up, "What plan?"

Everyone else in the room stared at him.

Grace was nonplussed. She went on, "In the event of his death or disability, every employee will receive ninety days severance pay. Unfortunately, that doesn't include any bonuses or overtime that may have been earned. We only have two open cases right now and after they are closed that will be that."

"That's more than fair," Willis said. Everyone else but Adams nodded in agreement.

"If however," Grace continued, "anyone was interested in taking the business over he laid out a plan where it could be purchased in installments." As she finished she looked at Tom again.

No one said anything for a while. Adams began looking around the room seemingly waiting for someone to pick up the ball and keep him employed.

Grace ended the silence. "That's about it. We can pick this up after the funeral. If you'll excuse me, I have to call Cal's ex and find out when she and his daughter are coming in." She stood up.

"Thanks for coming in." She looked at Willis. "Will you let me know if you talk to Travis?"

"Absolutely."

Grace went into Cal's office and shut the door. Adam's was still seated looking around the room. "This is awful," he said.

Willis nodded his agreement. "It is. I don't know about y'all but this is it for me. I've seen enough after twenty years with the police department and six with Cal. I'm gettin' too old for this shit."

Adams looked crestfallen. He glanced at Tom who was lost in his own thoughts.

Adams and Willis finally left the room to go to their own office. Sherry put her hand on Tom's shoulder and said, "Are you okay?"

"Yeah... just thinking."

"What are you going to do now?" she asked.

"I don't know."

She stared at him and he knew what she was getting at. "Don't worry, I'm not going on a vigilante spree."

She looked at him incredulously. "I have to finish up one of those two jobs Grace was referring to. And I am dead fucking serious Tom; if I find out you are lying to me I will shoot you myself."

He stood up and, despite everything, smiled. "C'mon Sher.' Give me some credit."

She thought of something and looked around the room to make sure they were still alone. She drew out her gun and offered it to him.

"Nope, not going to happen," he said putting up his hand.

"Take it."

"If anything happened to you while I was walking around with your gun I could never forgive myself."

"Please?" she pleaded.

"No Sherry. I won't. I'll be okay."

She holstered the gun and wiped her eye. "Asshole," she said.

He gave her a hug and said, "Thanks anyway."

"Still an asshole," she said into his shoulder.

Chapter 27

Tom Donovan couldn't help himself. As soon as Sherry had left him alone in the outer office he went over to Grace's desk and pulled out the phone book. This would have been a great time to have Brian Dinkle's assistance, but those days were over. He thumbed through the listings until he got to the S's, found what he wanted and ripped the page out.

The only thread he had to Mike Manzella was Mark Salerno. There were four listings for M. Salerno and two for Mark Salerno. He zeroed in on the two who were listed in North Buffalo, assuming that Salerno lived near his deceased great uncle. Neither one of these was guaranteed to be the right address; Salerno may be living with a relative, he struck Tom as the kind of guy who might still live with his mother for some reason, or he might not be listed at all. The landline telephone, much like the public payphone, seemed to be slipping into obscurity. Two addresses with no guarantee; not much, but right now it was all he had.

He slipped out of the office and made his way over to the North side. The first address was a double occupancy on Wallace Avenue. It was almost noon and the place looked empty. Tom got out of his car and strolled by the place and glanced up at it once he got close. The glassed-in front porch was filled with bikes and kid's stuff, so at least one of the flats was occupied by a family. He didn't see the red Mustang, but then he doubted he would see it again. If Salerno was in as deep as Tom thought he was, he was probably laying low. He decided to check the other address.

A few minutes later he pulled up in front of another double on Sterling. Again no Mustang. The asphalt siding was gray and the paint was flaking; Tom wondered if his landlord owned this place too. He was leaning forward looking through his windshield at the house when a young woman came out on the upstairs porch and lit a cigarette, struggling with her lighter in the cold breeze. Tom was just about to hop out of the car and call to her when a fist hit his driver's side window.

"Jesus Christ!" he said. He spun his head and saw Detective James Foster frowning down at him.

Another knock, this one not as loud, on the passenger side. It was Foster's partner, Ernie

Santiago and he didn't look too pleased either. Santiago pointed to the door and Tom popped the lock. Santiago slid in and glared at Tom.

"Did we scare ya?" Santiago began.

"Uh, yeah." He glanced in the rearview and saw Foster buttoning his coat headed back towards an unmarked Crown Victoria that Tom hadn't even noticed before. He cursed himself for being so sloppy.

"Good," Foster said he owed you from last week. Now, tell me, what the fuck do you think you are doing here Tommy?"

Tom closed his eyes and leaned back onto the head rest. He let Santiago go on.

"Do you think we aren't taking this seriously? Cal was eight years retired but he was still one of us."

"Ernie—"

"Shut the fuck up!" Santiago blurted. "We cut you some slack last week but that train has left the station. It's time for you to stand down and stay the fuck out of the way!"

Tom was embarrassed but at the same time he could feel his blood rising. He bit his tongue and stared straight ahead.

"I'm serious Tom. If I see you out here again before we get Manzella I will run you in myself."

"Okay," was all Tom could muster.

"Good, now go the fuck home." Santiago finished and got out of the car, slamming the door. He stood on the sidewalk and watched Tom drive all the way down to Linden and turn the corner.

>>><<<

Tom drove home with his tail between his legs. He didn't know what else he could do. Half of the Buffalo PD was probably out looking for Manzella and Salerno. He was alone, unarmed and in danger of pissing off the very people who were trying to help.

He got a bottle of water and sat down in the recliner and sulked. He felt helpless and he hated the feeling. He gazed around the apartment, focusing on nothing in particular, and then his eyes fell on his laptop on the dining room table. He went over and booted it up.

He logged on to his e-mail account and saw the two messages in his in box. The first one was from Brian Dinkle. It was basically a copy of the first e-mail Brian had sent the week before, revealing the sketchy information he had about Mr. Jones and the Sons of Eire. Tom had deleted the original but was pretty sure that the Feds could have retrieved it when they searched his computer. He hadn't really expected anything different.

The second e-mail was from Agent Miller and it had an Adobe Reader attachment. Tom opened it up and scanned it. He couldn't believe what he was reading so he read it again, this time paying attention to everything it said.

"Son of a bitch," he said out loud.

It was almost 4:00 PM. He picked up his cell phone and dialed Donovan's Tavern and Bonnie the bartender picked up.

"Bonnie I need to talk to Whitey," Tom said, foregoing the usual small talk.

"He's not here, sweetie. He left with Hugh about an hour ago."

"Did he say where they were going?"

"Um, something about Hugh's boat."

"Okay. Thanks."

Bonnie had started to say something else but Tom had already hung up. He really wanted to get his hands on a gun and Whitey Brennan was the only one who could get one for him with few questions asked. If he couldn't do anything about

Manzella he could sure as hell go to the Son's of Eire and confront McNally/ O'Connor with what he had just read. Knowing the secrets and lies that O'Connor had carried with him all these years would mean he was desperate. And the man who was usually with him, whom Tom had already had an altercation with, was probably involved too.

He tried Whitey's cell phone and it went to voicemail. He left an urgent message for Whitey to call him back. He dug a business card out of his wallet for Brennan Concrete, the business that Whitey's sons, Dan and Peter, ran. The woman who answered the phone said that the brothers were out on a job. Tom had his doubts as he looked out the window and saw that the wind had picked up and it was raining. He asked her for Dan or Pete's cell phone number and she said she couldn't give them out but would be happy to give them a message. Tom didn't feel like arguing with her. He grabbed his coat and headed for the door.

Back in the same spot where he had spied on the Son's of Eire previously, he looked through the rain at the front and side of the club. There were no cars in the parking lot and only Dominic's bicycle chained to a downspout near the back entrance. He waited about a half hour and then couldn't take it anymore.

He jogged across the street and tried the front door, locked. He went around the side of the building to the service entrance and pulled it open. He entered a kitchen that was shrouded in darkness. The only light in the room was from the emergency exit signs over the doors. He made his way towards the door to the bar and bumped into something hard with his hip. Finally he pushed the swinging door open and was in the bar room.

Nobody. The room was deathly quiet and looked deserted. He was just about to turn and go back through the kitchen when he heard a noise from behind the bar. He inched over and peered over the bar and saw Dominic lay on the floor with a gash on his forehead and a large knot forming underneath it. Tom went to the end of the bar, lifted the gate and went behind where the man lay.

He was about to check for a pulse when Dominic stirred. Tom knelt down next to him and lifted one of his eyelids to check his pupils. Dominic thrashed suddenly as he came to and knocked Tom's hand away.

"Take it easy," Tom said.

Dominic's eyes started to focus and he put his hand up to the lump on his forehead. "Ah... shit..."

"What happened?"

"What?" Dominic replied. He was still clearing the cobwebs.

"Who did this to you?"

Dominic put his head back on the dirty rubber mat on the floor. He closed his eyes and said, "Three big fuckers... one old guy and two younger ones."

"What did they want?"

"They took Seamus and Tim."

"Who?" Tom started and then realized that it was the Brennans who had snagged O'Connor and his cohort. He jumped up and found a reasonably clean bar towel and filled it with ice. He helped Dominic sit up and told him to hold the ice on his wound. He picked up the phone behind the bar and called for an ambulance and then let himself out the front door of the club.

He punched in Whitey's number again, and again it went to voicemail.

"Whitey, it's Tom. I know what you're doing but we need to talk before you do anything crazy. Call me back."

He started his car and thought about what Bonnie had told him. It was the only place he could think of where the Brennans might be.

Chapter 28

Hugh Donovan had a 1927 wooden Chris Craft speedboat that had belonged to his own father who allegedly bought it to run whiskey across Lake Erie from Canada during prohibition. Tom thought the boat hadn't been near the water in years. He had no idea why his grandfather kept it, other than the boat having some kind of sentimental value. When Tom was a boy he had seen the boat in storage in a building in Lackawanna and then his father told him they had moved it to a place off of Fuhrmann Boulevard. Tom had given up pestering his father and grandfather to take him out on the boat long ago. His grandfather had always been short with him when he brought it up.

Tom drove up and down Fuhrmann Boulevard looking for signs of life. The wind had picked up even more and the rain was coming off the lake in sheets. The lakefront was deserted. The spring had been harsh and uninviting to anyone looking for an early launch. On his fourth pass he saw an old sign that piqued his interest. It was a small wooden billboard with a broken light hanging over it that said *Murphy's Boat Works and Storage* with an arrow pointing towards a gravel driveway that led to a large metal building at the water's edge. Maybe? The connection was that Murphy had been his grandmother's maiden name. He knew Hugh had property all over the area and most of it was under somebody else's name. Tom cut his headlights and turned down the drive.

He pulled up to an eight-foot fence with barbed wire across the top. As he peered through the locked gate he didn't see any vehicles near the building, which stood about twenty-five yards away from his vantage point. Then he noticed a dim light coming from a lone window near one of the doors on the building's near side. As far as he could see there were no security cameras.

Tom went back to his car and got a thick hooded sweatshirt from his gym bag. The chain link fence was wet and slippery so he carefully scaled it and threw the sweatshirt over the barbed wire and then hoisted himself over that. He was just about clear when his trailing pant leg got caught on the wire and he lost his balance. The barb ripped through his jeans and he felt it go into his calf. He froze for a second and then managed to free his leg and swing it over the fence. He held on until he had himself turned the right way and then dropped to the ground.

The cut was deep but clean. He looked back towards the building, saw no movement and then jogged towards the building but away from the window. Even though his clothes were totally rain-soaked he could feel the warm blood running down into his shoe. He made it to the corner of the building and then went around the side. The building was the size of a large gymnasium and had tall overhead doors on the south side. He continued on to the back, the side facing the lake. Whitey Brennan's Cadillac and a full-sized pickup truck were parked by another entrance. The wind was roaring now and he knew as soon as he opened the door he would probably draw attention to himself. He looked around and saw no other way in. He put his hand on the knob and before he could turn it, the door swung inward and Peter Brennan was standing there.

Peter stood 6'3" like his father but was probably about fifty pounds heavier, most of it muscle. He favored his mother as far as his facial features went, with a fair complexion and an angular nose. His younger brother Dan was physically identical but had inherited his father's broad nose and ruddy complexion.

Peter let Tom come inside from the rain but blocked him from going any farther into the building.

"You don't want to be here Tommy," he said grimly.

"Pete, I have to talk to your dad. There's been a huge misunderstanding."

"Ah fuck! What are you doing here?" Whitey said emerging from behind his son.

Tom looked at Whitey and pleaded, "Whitey, you've got to stop what you're doing."

"And what am I doing?" Tom had never seen Whitey like this. He was typically affable and friendly but now he was scowling and his brow was covered with perspiration. Tom also noticed what he thought might be blood splattered on Whitey's forearms.

"I know you have McNally!" Tom yelled. "But he's not who you think he is."

Peter shot his father a quizzical look and then Whitey frowned and said, "What are you talking about lad?"

"I can explain. Just give me a minute."

Whitey thought for a moment and then said, "Alright. Come with me." Peter stood aside and Tom followed Whitey around a corner to the main part of the building.

There were all manner of boats lining either side of the large room. As they approached the center of the room Tom saw the two men, Gerry O'Connor and his accomplice from the Sons of Eire, tied to two chairs facing each other about fifteen feet apart. Drawing even nearer Tom saw a small table between the two men. On it was a bottle of whiskey and a one foot length of rubber hose with a chunk of lead in it that Tom had seen once behind the bar at the tavern. Under the table there was a large floor drain.

O'Connor was conscious but looked dazed. His right eye was swollen shut and there was blood coming from his left ear. His friend looked worse for wear. He seemed to be unconscious, with his chin on his chest and blood soaking the front of his shirt.

"Oh fuck," Tom said out loud.

"You shouldn't be here kid." Tom turned around to see his grandfather standing by the Chris Craft.

"Hugh, you've gotta stop this," Tom said.

Hugh shook his head. "You stubborn son of a bitch. We warned you. Whitey told you we would take care of this."

Tom gestured over his shoulder at the two captives. "You don't know what you're doing." He turned towards O'Connor and pointed directly at him. "This man's real name is Gerry O'Connor and he's not in the IRA, not anymore anyway."

"What? Where the hell did you get that?" Hugh said disbelievingly.

"From the FBI. He's not in exile from Northern Ireland. He's a snitch for the FBI."

Hugh turned pale and looked down. "Bullshit," he said with waning conviction.

"Hugh I've seen the file. In '82 O'Connor got picked up using a phony passport at Logan Airport in Boston. He was looking at extradition back to Ireland or Great Britain when he ratted out a group running guns and money from the States to the IRA. The ring was broken up and twenty of his fellow patriots are still rotting away in a British prison. The Feds shipped him to Arizona but he hated it so he left protective custody and settled in here. I don't know if it's irony or some kind of misplaced sense of guilt, but he picked the name Seamus McNally. The real Seamus Mcnally died in Long Kesh prison in '81."

O'Connor must have come around because he was stirring behind Tom and mumbling, "No... lies."

Tom looked at him. "Fuck you," he said.

He turned back to Hugh and went on, "Then in '87 O'Connor was involved in a hit and run while he was shit faced. The Feds were going to cut him loose when he came back with a fresh list of names of IRA members still in the states. The Feds got him out of it."

"I thought he was out of protective custody," Whitey said from behind Tom.

"Officially yes," Tom said turning slightly. "But they kept tabs on him until 9/11. Then their focus shifted to other things." "I know who he is," Hugh said regaining his resolve. "I've known since right after it happened that this cock-sucker is the one who killed Colleen. Your dad knew too. We just had no idea what an absolute piece of shit he was."

Tom turned towards the other man and said, "This is Timothy Mooney. He's O'Connor's cousin by marriage and a former U.S. Customs Officer in Boston. He got caught up in the passport scandal and got fired, then moved to Buffalo right behind his cousin."

"Motherfucker," Hugh said. "All these years he had me convinced."

Tom turned back to O'Connor and looked down at him. "He had a lot of people fooled."

"Not him Tommy," Hugh said. "Hank Loughran."

"Hank? I don't..." he stammered.

"Old Hank brought word from the Sons of Eire that if we made trouble we were all going to end up like your dad, you, your mother, Whitey and his wife and boys."

"What?"

Hugh reached up onto the gunwale of the Chris Craft and took down a paper bag. He went on, "Back in the day, Hank was neck deep in the bullshit that was going on down at the club. I never quite understood it. He was born here, he fought for his country, but he had a soft spot for these jackals for some reason." He reached into the bag and removed the .38 Smith and Wesson that had until recently been in Tom's possession.

"Where did you get..." Tom stopped and he looked at Whitey. He fit his neighbor's description and it made sense. "You broke into my apartment?"

Whitey looked down.

"On my instructions," Hugh said, getting Tom's attention back. "I already lost your dad, Tom. I couldn't have you running around half-cocked."

Tom blanched suddenly and said, "I guess it didn't matter to you that there is some half crazy drug dealer running around trying to kill me?"

Hugh frowned and shook his head. "Whitey said you were mixed up in something else. I had no idea." He shrugged then and walked directly in front of O'Connor who was now completely cognizant and aware of what was about to happen.

"Hugh, don't," Tom said.

O'Connor looked around Hugh at Tom. "Jesus it was an accident. There's not a day goes by that I don't regret what I done!" he yelled.

Tom took a step forward but Pete and Dan had crept up on either side of him and each one grabbed an arm with their thick calloused hands. He tried to break free but the brothers held fast.

"The FBI still checks on this guy. He can't wind up dead."

Hugh had started to raise the revolver but he lowered it and looked over his shoulder at his grandson. "If and when they ever find these cock-suckers, I'll be in the ground next to your grandma."

O'Connor wasn't finished pleading or dealing. He gestured with his chin toward Mooney and said, "I didn't kill your son! It was Mooney! Your boy followed me out to the lot and Mooney cold cocked him and put him in his car and then into the canal."

"That figures," Hugh said. "You're nothing but a rat and a coward and I didn't think you'd have the balls to take out my son."

There was a trace of relief on O'Connor's face as he thought he was getting through to Hugh. It all vanished when Hugh raised the gun again.

"But this is for Colleen."

"Wait!" O'Connor yelled just as the gun exploded. The bullet hit him right above his left eye and then took a chunk of the back of his skull as it exited. The recoil of the weapon almost knocked Hugh off his feet. His skin turned ashen and he looked like he might pass out.

"Shit!" Tom yelled.

Hugh regained his balance and composure. He looked at Whitey and growled, "Get him out of here."

Whitey led the way as his sons dragged a struggling Tom towards the door.

"Hugh! God damn it!"

They rounded the corner and the gun went off again. Outside the rain had stopped, but the wind was still pounding the shore and the dark sky made it seem later than it was. Tom had stopped struggling but the Brennans kept a firm grip on him just the same. They reached the gate and Whitey unlocked the padlock. Tom stepped through the opening and turned around to face Whitey.

"Do you know how fucked up this is?" He shouted above the wind.

Whitey looked contrite. He yelled back, "Tom, I'm sorry. You weren't supposed to be here. But you've got to let the old man have this. It's been eating away at him for years."

"I know it has. But he just invited a world of shit down on his head."

"He knows that Tommy. But he's thinking he's got nothing to lose."

"What are you talking about?" Tom asked.

"He was serious about joining your grandmother Tom. He's got late stage prostate cancer."

"How long..." Tom couldn't finish.

"He just found out. Doctor said he's got six months, tops."

"What about you Whitey? And Pete and Dan?" Tom said gesturing to his boys.

Whitey smiled slightly and said, "I owe your granddad debts that I could never pay in this lifetime."

Tom shook his head in frustration. "Nobody can owe somebody that much."

"Ah, you're wrong Tom. Someday I'll explain it to you."

"What about them?" Tom asked once again pointing to Whitey's sons.

"Were a package deal, Tom," Dan said, now more that ever resembling his father.

Whitey grew serious again. "Go home Tom," he said. "We have a little cleanup to do." Then he thought of something and reached into his coat and pulled Tom's missing Glock out of his belt. He handed it to Tom. "Sorry."

With that he re-locked the gate and the three men headed back towards the building.

Tom got in his car and as he was putting the gun into the glove compartment, suddenly felt the sting from the cut on his leg again. He rolled up the leg of his ruined pants and took a closer look. It was in the fleshy part of his calf but the blood had already started to coagulate. It looked like it could use a couple of stitches but he was in no mood for another trip to the emergency room and the questions that would come with it. He started the car and looked out the windshield to the top of his fence where his sweatshirt swayed wanly in the wind. He suddenly felt a wave of exhaustion wash over him and decided to leave it. With nothing else to do, he started the car and headed for home.

Chapter 29

Tom sat in the recliner with in a Buffalo Police Athletic League tee shirt and boxer shorts with his leg propped up. He had gotten home and stripped down and stood under the shower until the hot water ran out. He gingerly washed out the cut on his leg. It had started bleeding again briefly, but it didn't look too bad. He spread some disinfectant on it and covered it with a gauze pad and tape. On the table next to him was a bottle of Jameson and a tumbler next to the 9 mm Glock. He stared straight ahead into nothing.

It was over, the people responsible for the deaths of his sister and father were dead. He marveled at how seeing revenge delivered so brutally and after such a long time could make him feel so ambiguous about his sense of justice. He was angry at his grandfather for taking matters into his own hands but at the same time wondered if he hadn't been working towards the same end. Gerry O'Connor and Tim Mooney had been dealt with, never to be seen again. They were now just a memory being washed down the floor drain of a nondescript metal building at a boat yard.

And what of Hank Loughran and his tipping Tom off to the Sons of Eire? Was he trying to unburden himself of a secret he had been keeping for the last twenty-three years? People always had secrets, Tom knew, some darker and more dangerous than others.

The exertion, the whiskey and the stress of the last few days finally caught up with him and he drifted off in the chair.

Daylight in the room. Someone pounding at the door just outside the living room. Tom picked up the nine and put it behind his back and peeked through the curtain into the hallway.

It was Special Agent Miller. He was by himself and staring back at Tom through the window. Tom opened the door and Miller stormed into the room. Miller noticed the gun at Tom's side but it didn't seem to phase him in the least.

"What?" Tom said.

"You fucked me. I don't know how yet, but you fucked me," Miller responded. Tom noticed that even though Miller was in his usually impeccable FBI standard suit and tie, his face gave away the fact that he was under stress.

"What are you talking about?" Tom asked. He broke eye contact and walked over to the table and placed the gun down. He knew the half empty whiskey bottle and the gun probably didn't make him look like the most stable person but he didn't care.

"You tipped Dinkle off."

"Bullshit."

Miller took a step forward and got in Tom's face. "We know it wasn't the e-mail so it had to be the phone call. What was it? Was there a code word?"

"No," Tom lied. "I did exactly what you wanted. Are you telling me you didn't get him?"

Miller was fuming. "You know we didn't asshole! I just got off the phone with our Tampa field office. He was using a hijacked IP address and enough misdirection and booby traps to make it look real."

Tom shrugged. "I don't know what you expect me to say. I told you the stuff he was doing was over my head. I'm not the MIT grad in the room."

"Fuck you," Miller shot back.

"So he set up some innocent patsy in Florida?"

"Not exactly," Miller said through a combination of a frown and a smirk. "They raided some piece of shit trailer park in Plant City and the IP address belonged to a guy who was into child pornography."

Tom thought for a minute and then asked, "Do you think Dinkle set this guy up?"

"Doesn't look like it. It wasn't just the computer. There were pictures and DVD's all over the place. They said this guy looked like the King of the Perverts."

"Shit," Tom said.

"It's something the Digital Underground does when they aren't violating national security, outing pedophiles and other miscreants. I guess it makes them feel better about being a bunch of lawless, antisocial rejects."

Tom fought off a smirk. "Well, I don't know what to tell you."

Miller walked over towards the door and turned around. "I'm sure you don't. And if I didn't have to fly to DC to explain why we are two steps behind these assholes we would be continuing this conversation downtown."

Tom shrugged again and struggled not to say anything flippant.

Miller slammed the door on his way out. Tom knew he was really going to be angry when he eventually found out O'Connor had disappeared without a trace.

The signal for Brian had been for Tom to mention any song title from the music that he had loaded on the Mp3 player. Tom had used the phrase 'Bad Luck,' and Brian had known that Tom's phone and computer were being monitored and he would have to cover his tracks. The Mp3 player wasn't a problem any more. At Brian's suggestion it had been smashed and dropped down a storm drain.

He spent the rest of the day holed up in his apartment, thinking and reading and mindlessly flipping through the channels on his television. He called his uncle and when the call went to voicemail he declined to leave a message. After dinner Sherry Palkowski called and told him Cal's wake would be the following evening. He asked her if she wanted to ride with him, but she said that she had offered to take Grace, and Grace had accepted.

After sundown he grew restless. He kept checking the news websites for any word on the two missing men or the apprehension of Mike Manzella but came up empty. He wanted more immediate information so he grabbed the Glock and headed to the office. He let himself in and went to Brian's former office. All of Brian's computer equipment was gone leaving only dust outlines on his desk and side table. The metal storage cabinet was yawning open and Tom found what he was looking for, the police scanner. He took it home and turned it on and sat and listened. Some time after midnight he drifted off again.

Chapter 30

Tom arrived at the Carver Brother's Funeral home at 7:15 PM and the room was already overflowing. Most of the attendees were black with the exception of a few older white guys in suits, who looked like retired cops to Tom, and Cal's widow Grace. There were also a few active members of the force, turned out in their dress blues, looking solemn and speaking to each other in hushed tones.

Tom made his way over to the closed casket and Grace. She was putting up a brave front, greeting people and accepting their condolences, but Tom could see the pain behind her eyes. It occurred to him that he hadn't really got to know the Fredericksons that well in the time that he had worked for them. He did know that they had been married for some time and were deeply devoted to each other. It was a rare kind of timeless, easy affection that not all that many people shared after a long-term relationship. It was the same kind of love that he had recognized in his own parent's marriage.

She smiled at him and accepted a kiss on the cheek. After their conversation the day before Tom didn't know how else to express his grief so he got out of the way of the people lined up behind him waiting to express their sympathy.

He saw Sherry across the room talking to a well-dressed black woman in her fifties. The woman smiled and said something to Sherry and then turned to say something to a younger woman standing behind her. Tom caught Sherry's eye and they met half- way.

"That was Cal's ex and his daughter," Sherry said quietly.

Tom glanced over to the two women who were now talking to one of the uniformed policemen. "Until yesterday I didn't even know he had an ex, or a daughter."

Sherry looked over their way too and said, "He didn't talk about it much. They got divorced when his daughter was ten and they moved down south."

Tom turned back to Sherry. "He didn't have any pictures or anything in his office did he?"

"Just one old one of the daughter. I guess the break-up was kind of messy."

Tom thought about that. Everybody he knew seemed to have something in their past that they had a hard time dealing with.

"Did you see Grace?" Sherry asked, bringing him back to the present.

"Yeah."

"I don't know how she does it."

"I know, I remember my mom trying to be brave and gracious while a bunch of strangers and people she hardly knew were tramping all over the house loading up on free sandwiches and potato salad." Tom immediately felt a pang of guilt for comparing some one else's grief to his own.

Sherry looked like she might tear up now. "And to think it's the second time."

"Wait... what?" Tom said weakly.

She looked him in disbelief. "You didn't know?"

"I had no idea."

She took his arm and led him to the side of the room and dropped her voice down to a whisper. "Grace's first husband was a cop. He got killed in a shootout in '84."

"Jesus, and she married another cop?"

Sherry shook her head. "No, they met when Cal was still on the job. She told me that she wouldn't marry him until he retired."

This made Tom feel even worse. The revelation that Grace had already lost a husband to a violent death and years later met a man whom she wouldn't marry until she was sure he would have a safer way to make a living compounded the guilt he felt. The knowledge that he kept dragging other people into his screwed-up existence was devastating.

Sherry was still talking but Tom couldn't hear what she was saying. When she paused he excused himself and went to the men's room.

He was splashing water on his face by the sink when someone came in behind him.

"You okay?" It was Simon Willis.

"Yeah... this sucks though," Tom said reaching for a paper towel.

Willis nodded and walked over towards a urinal. "That it does." He paused while he did his business. When he was done and zipped up he made his way over to the sink and looked at Tom in the mirror. "You gonna be okay?"

After a moment Tom threw the towel in the wastebasket and said, "Yeah."

"I know you blame yourself Tom, but Cal knew the risk. He was armed and ready. You were on the job long enough to know that all it takes is one short moment of inattention and the shit will hit the fan."

"I know, but it was supposed to be me."

"It wasn't though. It wasn't your turn."

Tom looked at Willis incredulously, "You're not going to give me the 'Hand of Fate' bullshit are you?"

"Nah," Willis said turning on the tap. "I been around long enough to know that destiny can be altered with a little effort." He looked at Tom again as he reached for a towel. "Let me ask you something."

"Go ahead."

"If it had been the other way around, would you have done the same thing for Cal?"

After a brief pause Tom said, "Yeah, probably."

Willis straightened his tie. "I thought so. And I know Cal thought so too. He wasn't the kind to go around pumping up people's egos, but I know he had a lot of respect for you."

Tom fell silent. Willis walked by him and clapped him on the arm. "You want to make amends? Don't let the anger and the sorrow stop you from being a good man. That's the way Cal lived." Willis was half way out the door when Tom called out to him.

"Simon, is Travis here?"

Willis glanced back. "Nope, he finally called me back yesterday and said he's alright, and that I should call off the dogs and stop hasslin' his friends. The boy is taking it hard I guess." Then Willis was gone.

Tom spent another hour at the wake, mostly near Sherry, not saying much but nodding a few hellos to a few of the faces he recognized. At 8:30 the room was still full and Grace was still politely talking to a line of people so Tom said goodnight to Sherry and headed for the door.

He was numb now, overwhelmed by the emotions he was feeling, loss, anger, gratitude and a few others under the surface. As he pulled out onto Delavan he was pulled out of his reverie by a shadow moving in a car parked on the street. Was he paranoid or had his sense of alarm been heightened over the events of the last few days? Sure enough the car pulled out into traffic one car behind him.

Just to check, instead of proceeding down to Bailey Avenue and making a right turn towards home he made an abrupt left and accelerated down a side street. After a beat, the gray sedan turned in behind him and picked up speed. In the fading, overcast daylight he thought he saw the driver put a phone up to his ear.

Right down another side street and then a left onto Bailey, this time a little faster. The gray sedan accelerated behind him. As nonchalantly as possible, Tom glanced at the locked glove box and thought about the Glock inside it. He knew who was following him and what he wanted. He knew it was going to end tonight.

Chapter 31

Tom sped down Bailey with the sedan close behind. Once it got close enough that he positively recognized Mike Manzella barely disguised with a pair of glasses and a ball cap. Manzella was still barking into his phone.

A quick right onto Walden Avenue and then a right onto Goembel Avenue, a narrow side street of one family homes, half of which were either condemned or close to it. The city had been tearing down properties or chasing down the absentee landlords to do it. Every third lot on Goembel seemed to be missing a home. The street was a testament to the hard times that had befallen the neighborhood.

There was a car coming from the other direction. It wasn't a red Mustang but Tom was pretty sure he knew who it was. There were two of them now. Tom's only ace in the hole was that he was on familiar ground. He saw what he was looking for, veered left and then slammed on the brakes and put the car in park.

He heard the car behind him come to a stop from what sounded like twenty or thirty feet away. He unlocked the glove box, took out the Glock and rolled out of the driver's side.

He ran and waited for the shooting to start. Nothing yet. He made it up the cracked, weed-strewn driveway between the two boarded-up houses and turned left. The back door of the house was padlocked but one good kick and the rotting wood on the doorjamb splintered and he was inside. He made his way through the kitchen, the only light in the house was the fading daylight coming through the plastic and plywood covered windows. He knew he had picked the right house. Four years before he and Joe Walczak had chased an eighteen year old crack dealer into the same home and found him in the attic crawl space.

As he crept up the stairway in the middle of the house he heard the two men enter the kitchen. Salerno was speaking in a whisper and Manzella was telling him to shut up. Tom made to the top and went into a small bathroom at the rear of the house. He found a discarded forty-ounce bottle that had been left by some squatter or junkie and heaved it down the hall. The bottle hit the doorway at the end of the hall but didn't break.

Silence now. Tom stepped back inside the bathroom and waited. He pulled the gun out of the waistband of his suit pants and checked the action on the slide as quietly as possible. He leveled the gun towards the top of the stairs and his stomach tuned over. "Fuck," he said to himself. He was sure that he had subconsciously convinced himself that he wouldn't be able to point a weapon at another human being in anger. Now it was go time and he couldn't do it. Time for plan B.

He tucked the gun back into his waistband and turned around. In the back corner of the bathroom where the bathtub used to be was a hole in the floor, left there by the copper thieves who had been vandalizing vacant homes for years. Tom took off his jacket, threw it down and lowered himself carefully through the floor joists. He heard footsteps reach the top of the stairs and looked down, it was still a good two foot drop to the floor underneath him. The chance of a stealthy landing were pretty remote. He would have to land and be ready to move.

He let go and dropped. The floor underneath him sounded like it was going to give way on impact but it held. He rushed to the door and as he cleared it he came face-to-face with Mark Salerno. Salerno looked shocked and terrified, despite the fact that he had a chrome .22 in his hand. Tom saw his opportunity and rushed Salerno full on. He planted his shoulder into Salerno's chest and sent him flying backwards and through the open door to the basement.

Salerno cried out and then was drowned out by the sound of breaking wood as the stairs he landed on gave way. For a moment after there was silence and then Salerno cried out again. "Mike! Mike... I can't move."

Hearing footsteps on the stairs, Tom retreated to the kitchen and ducked around the corner.

"Fuck! Mike... Jesus, help me!"

From his hiding place Tom heard Manzella at the top of the basement stairs, "Shut the fuck up you..."

Tom had come around the corner and Manzella heard him and was starting to turn. Before Manzella could raise his gun, Tom grabbed his wrist and slammed Manzella's gun hand into the wall. Manzella held tight to the gun and brought his knee up towards Tom's groin. Tom managed to turn in time and Manzella's knee struck him in the thigh. It hurt like hell but not nearly as bad as it would have if Manzella had been on target. Manzella brought his left hand up to Tom's face. The bandage was gone but the scar where his pinkie had once been still looked raw. With his right hand Tom hit Manzella hard in the ribs, knocking the air out of him. He saw an exposed nail sticking out of the wall and pulled Manzella's gun hand down over it. Manzella grunted and the gun came loose and tumbled away out of reach. Manzella's breath felt hot in Tom's face as he marshaled the will to push himself and Tom off of the doorjamb.

Tom planted a foot and used their momentum to spin Manzella around towards the kitchen. Manzella was still trying to regain his balance when Tom's right hand flashed and caught Manzella in the eye. The thug wobbled backwards but Tom stayed on him. He grabbed the front of Manzella's jacket with his left hand and swung his right hard again, this time he heard the man's nose break. Manzella spun and went down on his hands and knees and was crawling towards the back door. Tom let him reach the doorway and then kicked him in the rear end as hard as he could. Manzella rolled down the step and out onto the damp ground.

Tom sucked in air and tried to catch his breath. He heard Salerno yelling something about rats as he stepped out of the house and bent over

Manzella. He was reaching for his gun when a pair of rough hands pulled him back and threw him backwards into a wall. His head hit first and he saw stars and then nothing for a moment. When his vision became slightly less blurry he was aware of the young black man with a forearm pressed into his throat and a big silver automatic pointed in his face. In his condition he wasn't sure, but he thought he had seen the kid before. He was a member of the Street Kings.

There was another man standing over Manzella, also armed. Manzella slowly rolled over and looked at the gun pointing at him. Despite the circumstances he regained his bravado.

"You spooks are making a big fucking mistake," he said as he put his hand on his disfigured nose.

"Shut the fuck up!" the man standing over him said.

"When the people I work for find out about this you guys are fucked."

"Nah, we good," a new voice said.

Cal's nephew, Travis Parker, had emerged from the side of the house carrying a Colt .45 with a suppressor attached.

"Travis..." Tom said weakly.

Travis looked at Tom and put a finger to his lips. He looked back at Manzella and said, "See, we already talked to the Bull and we're tight now."

Manzella turned white at the mention of the Bull, a name Tom hadn't heard before.

"Bullshit!" Manzella sputtered.

"Nah, you out of a job, motherfucker."

"I want to talk to him." Manzella was losing steam and had begun to plead. "If he tells me himself I'll believe it."

Travis smiled grimly and took a step over towards the man. "That ain't gonna happen."

"Fuck you nigger. We're working for the same people!"

"Well, we might have been, but you went and made this personal." Travis fired the gun into Manzella's chest and Manzella looked shocked. Then Travis bent over and from about a foot away put another round into his forehead.

From inside the house they could still hear Salerno, although his voice had faded to a kind of animalistic moan.

Travis turned towards Tom and said, "Where're your keys Tom?"

"What?" Tom's head was spinning and he was losing focus.

"Your car keys? Where are they?"

"Coat pocket, upstairs bathroom."

Travis gestured to the other man and they both went inside the house. The man watching Tom took a step back and he slid down the wall.

"What the fuck is wrong with you?" the man asked.

A gun fired once inside the house and then three more times in rapid succession. Travis and his associate came out of the house and Travis handed his keys to the man behind him.

"Help me get him to his car," he said. "Meet me down on Sussex."

"Fuck T'," one of the men said. "Why don't we just leave him here?"

Travis glared at the man, shutting him up.

Tom's memory of the ride to the hospital would be hazy at best. But he would remember Travis calmly driving as if nothing had happened.

"What did you do?" Tom slurred.

"Just cleanin' up a little."

"Shit Travis, what happened to you going straight? Law school?"

"And do what?" Travis shook his head. "Play by the rules and hope somebody hands me a job. Fuck that Tom. Shit was never going to happen."

"No, you don't know that."

"You played by the rules. My uncle played by the rules. How the fuck did that turn out?" Travis was becoming agitated.

Tom fell silent the rest of the way. As they pulled into the emergency room entrance he had one last question. "Is it true? What you said about this Bull guy?"

Travis pulled the car to the curb and pulled up his hood. He shot Tom a quick look and said, "Take care of yourself, Tom." He opened the door and walked quickly away into the night.

It took a few minutes but a security guard came out of the building and knocked gently on the passenger side window.

"Hey, you can't park here. We need to leave this clear for the ambulances."

Tom looked at the officer. He tried to speak but nothing came out. He fumbled for the door latch, opened it and fell out of the car.

Chapter 32

The first time he came to, Donovan was aware he was in a dark room. After looking around a bit he realized that it was daytime outside as a few slivers of light were seeping in past the room darkening shades. He checked his body next and found the IV needle in his arm and the bandage on his head.

Slowly it came back to him. Loughran, Manzella, Cal and all the other souls who had fallen by the wayside the last few weeks. He brought up their faces in his mind and checked them off one by one.

His mother. He had to tell her he was okay. He strained his eyes in the darkness and couldn't see a phone in the room. He tried to sit up in his bed and heard a buzzer go off on a monitor next to him.

A sliver of light as the door to the corridor opened and a nurse came in. She moved a switch on the wall up and the room brightened slightly.

"Mr. Donovan, you need to lay down," she said quietly but with urgency.

"Where am I?" he asked hoarsely.

"You're in the Neurology ward at ECMC." She put a hand on his shoulder and gently pushed him back into bed.

"My mother..."

"Your family has been notified and can see you when the doctor clears it."

"When..." his voice trailed off and he went under again.

The next time he opened his eyes it was only slightly less dark and he was aware of someone standing over him.

"Hey kid." It was his Uncle Sam.

Tom opened his eyes and tried to clear his head.

Sam tried to smile but it didn't quite work. He looked down at his nephew and said nothing.

"Mom?" Tom rasped.

"She's fine. She's going to be staying with us for a while. As a matter of fact your aunt and I are trying to convince her to sell the house and make it permanent."

"Did she come?"

Sam grimaced. "Here? No. I didn't want her to see you like this. When you get up and around I'll bring her in."

Tom was angry that his uncle had made that decision on his own, but then he remembered how angry he had been the last time they had spoken. He had wondered if they would ever speak again. For now he bit his tongue.

"Sorry," Tom mumbled, closing his eyes.

His uncle patted his arm and said, "Tom, I'm not your dad and I know sometimes I have tried to act like I was. When you get out we'll have you come over for dinner and try to get back to normal."

"Normal, that's funny," Tom said.

Sam gave a slight smile and said, "Well, our version of normal anyway."

Two days later he was being released. He was still groggy but had been told that there wasn't any permanent damage. However, if he were concussed again it could be life altering. Once again his car had been impounded by the Buffalo PD and he had been questioned about the events at the house on Goembel Avenue. He had lied again- it seemed to be getting easier for him to do so- and told the detective he had recognized a few members of the NBH, the Street King's biggest rival. He did tell them about hearing a conversation about someone called "the Bull" and told them he might be someone of interest.

They wouldn't have let him drive even if he had a car and he was just about to ask one of the nurses to call a cab when Sherry walked in.

"You ready?" she said.

"You bet your ass I'm ready."

She pushed him out of the entrance in a wheelchair and then ordered him to wait while she got her car. The weather had finally warmed and the hazy sunlight hurt his eyes.

"I appreciate this Sher'," he said as they pulled onto Grider Street.

"No worries. I'm sure you would do the same for me if I'd been shot at, beaten and dumped on the curb."

He put his head back and smiled. The reality of his situation kept coming back to him however. He had lost his father a long time ago. It had turned out that Hank Loughran, a father figure to him, had been carrying his dark secrets around with him for years and had betrayed his family's trust and his father's memory. The only thing he would never know was whether Hank knew about O'Connor's lie or had been taken in too. And now Cal was gone, not so much a father figure, but a mentor and someone who had taken a chance on him when he couldn't even get a job as a security guard at the mall.

And Colleen, he vaguely remembered having a dream about his late sister while he was under. In the dream it wasn't her as the child he remembered; she was an adult. She was alive and beautiful, but in the dream she had seemed troubled. That was all he could remember. The dream had faded like his memory of her had been doing for so long.

And unless she had visited him while he was unconscious, Erica had stayed true to her word and was truly done with him. Not that he could blame her. She was better off that way.

"So, what are you going to do?" Sherry interrupted his thoughts.

"Hmm. I don't know. Take the buyout I guess." He paused. "I guess that's taking money from a grieving widow though, isn't it?"

"If I know Grace, she'll insist. This was Cal's plan Tom."

He looked out the window at the people on the street, carrying on with the everyday.

"I've still got my PI ticket. I guess I could freelance, see how that works."

"You can make that work if you want it to." She was trying to sound convincing. "We all have to move on I guess."

He thought about what Simon Willis had said about letting go of the anger and the misery that life offered up.

He looked back at his friend and said, "Yeah, what else can you do?"

I am deeply thankful to several people who helped me with this book. My friend, Cynthia Lehman who edited the manuscript, (exhausting several red pens in the process) whose patience and suggestions helped turn my ramblings into a coherent story.

Mark Pogodzinski and the people at No Frills Buffalo for shepherding a novice through two books now. It's been invaluable to find someone like them to help turn a whim into a dream then into a book.

I had the pleasure of meeting and working with a very talented local artist, Valerie Eddy, whose imagination and creativity are responsible for the cover of the book. You can check out more of Valerie's work at diversifyadvertise.com

And finally, my family: My mother, who along with my late father instilled a love of reading in all nine of their children. Mom, no surprise, is also my biggest supporter. My wife Jeanne daughter Emily, always politely listening to me drone on about "the process." And my youngest Elizabeth, your unflinching love and honesty are always welcome.

DCC

25388050R00171

Made in the USA
Middletown, DE
28 October 2015